The Sweet Scent of Liver

Eli Wilde

Also by Eli Wilde

Cruel

Two Lumps of Sugar for Mr Anxiety

Contents

Rêve Noir

Adel watched them cross the street. The mother and father walked hand in hand, like dreamers still in love. Their young son piggy backed on the mother's shoulders. She stared in their direction a long time after they were gone. Even though she longed for a child of her own, she had made up her mind to never have any. How could she be a mother with an ugly past like hers?

She crossed the Seine over Petite Pont and walked along Rue Saint-Jacques heading for Rue Dante and the apartment block where the Englishman, Sykes, lived. There was an elevator inside, but Adel hated elevators and climbed the six flights of stairs to Sykes' apartment, counting the steps as she did. One step for every mistake she had made in life.

There were not enough steps.

Once outside his door, she rang the doorbell. He answered immediately, like always, as if he had been waiting behind the door for her to arrive.

Sykes kissed Adel on each cheek. She held her breath as he did, not wanting to take in his old man scent. He beckoned her inside and led her to the expansive lounge. The air inside the apartment was cool and airy, a welcome contrast to the Parisian summer outside. She sat on the couch opposite Sykes. He poured her lemon tea while he spoke.

"I want to try something different today, Adel," Sykes said in a Geordie accent that did not match his upper-class persona.

Adel looked out the window, staring at Notre Dame's steeples, thinking about what she would do if she owned an apartment with a fabulous view like that.

"Everyone is bored with sex. Sex is yesterday's turn on," Sykes continued.

"What do you mean?" Adel asked, suddenly interested in what Sykes had to say.

"I mean my clients, and just about everyone else, want to experience more than a cheap sexual thrill. They want to experience darkness."

"Darkness isn't something I want to experience."

Sykes interlaced his finger in front of his face. "Don't be nervous. We are still talking about dream sequencing here. It is still fantasy, but instead of erotic dream sequencing, we are now set up for dark dream sequencing."

"You're not convincing me this is the right way to go."

Sykes smiled. "As you know, it is the set up that makes this whole business work. Instead of using individuals who are sexually orientated, we now use individuals who are a lot deeper."

"Psychopaths and killers, you mean?"

"At first, that's exactly the type of person our clients wanted their dream hosts to represent. Surprisingly, psychopaths don't dream much, even when influenced by the serum. They are quite boring. And although killers, at first, appeared capable of supplying the dark horror we were looking for, they soon became predictable. It's all slash and burn with them."

"I take it you have found a suitable dream host for this new darkness fix?"

"Yes, we have a host; it happened quite by chance. When you think about it, though, it's so obvious it makes you wonder why we didn't consider it in the first place."

"Who is the host?"

"A priest who has lost his faith in God. Don't get me wrong. He still believes in God; he just doesn't agree with God's word anymore. That's what makes him perfect for dark dream sequencing. He is close to both God and Satan. He believes in both yet follows neither."

"A priest doesn't belong in this industry."

"That's where you are wrong. He is the same as you, he needs the money. In truth, when he first came to us, we saw him as a charity case. We didn't see him as host material. As soon as we looked inside his head, everything changed."

"What did you see inside his head?"

"A potent mix of confusion, guilt, and sin. It makes for fascinating viewing."

"I'm a sex fantasist, not a darkness whore. I don't do horror."

"As much as anything, this is for you, Adel. I know about your nightmare. I have seen it in your dreams. I want to erase that particular nightmare from your mind by showing you true darkness, horror that will make your own nightmare go away forever."

Adel didn't want to think about her nightmare. Nothing was private in this industry, but she was still annoyed with Sykes for mentioning it. "What about the observers?"

"What about them?"

"If you're doing this for me, I take it they will not be present to watch?"

"Dream sequencing is an expensive business. I can't do this without their support."

"I don't want to introduce any more horror into my life."

"The market has dropped out of the dream sequencing sex industry. I'm not sure you can make a living out of it anymore. I am not sure I can either. We both need to diversify."

"I don't have a choice, you mean?"

"You always have a choice. You can always say no."

Adel knew she could not say no, just like she knew Sykes thought the same thing. There was no other work for a nineteen-year-old without any qualifications. There was no work for anyone these days that did not involve exploitation.

"Come. It's time," Sykes said, standing and holding out his hand to Adel. "You were always my favourite. I know you will be fabulous at this."

The theatre was in the loft. Sykes rented the loft from the building owner and converted it three years ago, in response to the lucrative dream sequencing market. Although there were numerous public dream sequencing theatres throughout the city, it was the small, private theatres which generated the most interest from wealthy clients. These individuals wanted only the best hosts and dream fantasists. In Paris, there was no better dreamer than Adel.

When she stepped into the theatre, Adel was surprised to see the priest lying on the host bed, already prepared.

He slept soundly.

"What's he called?" Adel asked.

"Thomas Durant."

"Why was he prepared before me?"

"He was fretful when he arrived, he wanted to sleep immediately, that's all."

"Is he going to be okay for the procedure?"

"Stop worrying and get ready."

Adel made a move to remove her clothes.

"That is no longer necessary," Sykes said. "Just lie down and I will prepare you."

Adel hesitated. Something didn't feel right. Dream sequencing never felt right. She lay down on the bed next to Durant and Sykes covered her with a single, white bed sheet before fitting the neuro-imaging band to her head. He then attached the imager to the relay station which connected her to Durant and the four observation booths located behind the soundproof walls, opposite the two beds.

Adel had never seen any of the observers who watched her dreams. She had never wanted to see them.

"Are you ready?" Sykes asked.

Adel nodded.

Sykes injected Adel with the serum and a moment later, she was sleeping.

She awakened inside Thomas Durant's dream. Though she shared his dream, unlike a normal dream state, Adel was aware of everything she experienced like it was happening for real. The serum was initially developed by a pharmaceutical giant as a different kind of euthanasic, after it became socially and politically acceptable for individuals to choose the exact moment they wanted to die. It was supposed to induce euphoria before death. During trials with lower doses of the serum, researchers found that it induced incredibly real-istic dream states without any apparent side effects. A brain surgeon took the experiments one step further when he coupled the serum with neuro-imaging technology and made it possible for people to not only share their dreams with each other, but also make it possible for observers to watch dreams via 3D monitors. And so, dream sequencing was born.

The first thing Adel noticed inside Durant's head was the heat. Wildly intense, it felt like every inch of her skin was being burned by a lifetime of cigarette ends. As the neuro-imager began to feed pictures of Durant's dream into her mind, Adel saw that she was inside a cell. The wet, rusted metal walls of the cell matched the rusted bars on the door. She tried to move, to crawl towards the door-way, but her muscles were dead. Her body weight pinned her to the concrete floor like she was glued to it. She could barely breathe the hot air inside the cell. Her lungs ached violently as she gasped for a breath that was not there. Staring at her arms, she was appalled to see them blister as her skin burned away from her flesh. As the heat intensified, she could bear no more and passed out.

Adel awakened inside Durant's dream, still burning, to the sound of wailing. She was no longer alone. A hunched, humanoid like creature sat opposite her, clearly distressed. It was twice her size and moved its head from side-to-side as it moaned. Gristle-like shards grew from its entire body. Worse, the left side of its head was ripped open and pulled apart.

When it saw Adel was awake, it crawled towards her and started to bite her fingers with the teeth on the right side of its mouth. Adel screamed, but there was little air inside her lungs and only a whimper came from her lips. Unable to move, she could do no more than watch the creature as it chewed off her fingers, one by one.

"We need to leave this place," a male voice murmured from the other side of the doorway.

Adel looked towards the voice and saw a man staring back. Like her, the man had suffered from the heat. His smouldering skin glistened red and only half of his right arm remained. His nose and ears were missing too. Adel was not sure if it was because they had burned away or if they had been chewed off by a creature similar to the one chewing on her fingers. The pain in her hands was immense, but it was no match for the burning.

"Durant?" Adel managed to say.

"Yes."

"You crazy fuck. Get us out of here."

"I don't know how to do that," Durant said.

Adel wanted to close her eyes, but she no longer had eyelids. She stared beyond Durant and saw a cell identical to the one she was trapped inside. A man was sandwiched between two creatures performing hideously sexual acts on him. Neither the creatures, nor the man, looked like they were enjoying the experience, and each wailed as if they were in intense pain.

Adel had only experienced a chemical droplet fall inside her brain once before, when a host died. Durant was not dead, but when the droplet landed this time, the cell was no more and the heat vanished. She almost passed out again with the shock of no longer feeling any pain.

She was sitting on a bench in the middle of a school playground. A small boy, no more than six or seven years old, sat next to her. Other children circled the bench and from time to time, they would bend down and flash their phones in front of the boy. Adel didn't need to see the phones to know what images were on the screens. She knew the children were showing the little boy pictures of his mother. His mother, with a man who was not his father. Lots of men who were not his father. All the men were ugly and old. All of them were copulating with his mother.

"Make them stop, Mummy," the boy said, turning towards Adel and weeping. "Make them stop and tell me it's not true."

Adel hugged the boy and whispered, "Durant, get me out of here."

They were back in the hot place, in a labyrinth of tunnels with jagged walls, as if crooked teeth had gnawed them into existence. The heat was oppressive, but not as intense as it had been in the cell. Durant sat beside Adel. They were propped up against the tunnel wall, unable to move because of the weight of the air pressing them down. Both looked like their whole bodies had been scorched with a blow torch. Pieces of their body parts were missing.

"Was that your son?" Durant asked, barely audible.

Adel heard screams come from every tunnel opening around her. "No," she said, wincing at the pain in her dry throat as she spoke. "He is my nightmare, the son I will never have."

"Why did you take us to him?"

"I don't know. We are supposed to remain in the host's dreams, your dreams. Sometimes, on rare occasions, a transfer into the dream wanderer's head occurs."

Two creatures, with what looked like splinters of bone protruding from their necks and face, approached them. They moaned like they were in as much pain as the woman they held between them. Her bare flesh scraped against the wall as she was dragged along the tunnel, and into a hollow, where they disappeared. The woman's screams were lost inside the screams of innumerable others who suffered along with her.

"Where are we?" Adel asked. "What are those creatures?"

"This is my nightmare," Durant said. "A place shown to me by someone I no longer worship. The creatures who inhabit this place are called sharded. They are a nightmare waiting to be unleashed upon humanity."

Another sharded came running out of one of the tunnels. It held onto its head with both its hands and crashed from wall to wall, wailing as it rushed past them.

"Why do they look as tormented as us? Surely this is the one place where they should feel at home."

"There is no ease for anyone or anything in this place. It is meant to torment both human and sharded alike."

Adel wept through eyes that, again, had no eyelids. "You're the host, for God's sake. Take us someplace else."

"I can't."

"Why not?"

"I don't know any other place."

"You know Paris."

"Not in my dreams. I can only see this place when I sleep, nowhere else. Can't you take us away from here like you did before?"

"I already told you, only the dream host can control the places we see. We can only enter my dreams through a glitch in the system. Something to do with the flow of chemicals within the brain."

A finger pushed out of the ground next to Adel's leg as she spoke. It wriggled further out of the red soil and another finger appeared alongside it. A moment later, the fingers were joined by a hand, and then an arm. The hand crawled towards Adel's leg until a shoulder appeared and then, the fragmented head of a sharded. Seeing Adel, the sharded grabbed hold of her leg and as she looked down at it, she noticed her foot was missing.

The sharded pulled her along the floor towards the hole it crawled from, and she could do nothing but stare back at it.

"I want to go to Notre Dame," Adel yelled. "Take me to Notre Dame, Thomas, please."

"I can't."

"Yes, you can, just imagine we are there, and we will be."

"I can't remember what it looks like, all I know is this place."

The sharded pulled Adel's lower body into the ground.

"Forget about how it looks, think about how it feels. How it smells. Something about the cathedral that made you feel euphoric. There must be something!"

The sharded pulled so hard on Adel's leg that it broke her thigh bone in half. She silently screamed and tried to push the creature, but the air was too heavy and her muscles too weak. The sharded pulled again and her other leg snapped in half. It wrapped her legs around its arm and pulled her beneath the scorching soil until only her head and left arm remained above the surface. She stared wildly at Durant as the sharded pulled the rest of her beneath the surface.

And then, she sat on a bench, next to Durant, inside Notre Dame. She took in a lungful of air, then another. All the heat had vanished. All the pain too. She wanted to weep. Instead, she continued to breathe in the cool air of the cathedral.

"How did you do it?" she asked once she was settled. "What did you remember?"

"I remembered the sound of my footsteps echoing around the empty space when I was alone in the cathedral at the end of each day."

"Tell me about that hot place."

"You really want to know?"

"Yes, I do."

"I was taken there by God, six months ago."

"In a dream?"

"It didn't feel like a dream at the time. One minute I was here saying mass, the next, I was inside a pit of fire, burning alongside thousands of other people. Then, I awakened on the floor of the cathedral. I had been unconscious for only a minute or so. It felt like I had been away for days."

"Did God speak to you?"

"Not in the sense you are thinking. He speaks in a more visual way, by placing images inside your mind."

"What did he say to you? Why did he take you there?"

"He wanted to show me the fate of sinners so that I could warn those who cared to listen."

"Did you warn anyone?"

"No, I didn't. After I returned, I no longer believed in God's ways. I think He is insane. What other explanation is there for creating a world where sinners are exiled to an everlasting afterlife in unbearable pain? And by sinners, I mean those who do not follow the word of God. A sinner could be a perfectly loving mother who has done nothing but care for her children all her life without hurting another soul. Yet because she did not believe in God, she spends eternity burning in a place of His making, being tormented by demons who are tormented by life in that place. Does she really deserve to spend thousands of years after thousands of years screaming in a place like that? I can't see the sense in it after seeing that place with my own eyes and experiencing its pain."

"I've never believed in God."

"You need to start believing, He is real. You have some choices to make, choices that will determine how you spend your afterlife."

"I need to start believing in God, so I don't end up burning in Hell?"

"Not only do you need to believe in Him, you need to worship Him and follow His word. If you do not, the hot place awaits."

"You're telling me to worship God, not because it's the right thing to do. I should worship Him because I'll go to Hell if I don't?"

"Yes."

"That's fucked up."

"It is His way."

"What about you? If you no longer believe in His word, you know exactly what that means."

"I have no choice. Since He showed me His hell, I can't follow His word anymore."

"Even though you know what awaits you?"

"It is like I have no choice. My spirit has turned away from God. I can no longer endure Him or His ways."

Notre Dame began to fade from the peripheral of Adel's vision and she recognised the dream shift. "Thomas, for God's sake, concentrate," she yelled, but it was too late. The cathedral vanished and the hot place returned.

"I can no longer live," Durant said.

They were hanging upside down in a monstrous cavern with numerous other men, women, and children. Intense pain coursed through Adel's body. She was suspended by a metal rod that had been spiked through both her ankles. The pain felt even more sickeningly extreme seeing what had been done to her. Hundreds of thousands of people lay before them, writhing on the ground, as the sharded inflicted torture and torment upon them.

"I injected myself with a dose of serum before Mr Sykes injected me with the dose for this dream sequence," Durant said in a strained voice.

"If you took two doses of the serum, you will never awaken," Adel managed to say. "This place will become your reality when you die."

"It is already my reality. Once you find this place, it never leaves you."

A sharded creature approached. It had three heads that were no more than skulls with gaping maws. Six arms jutted from its body at awkward angles. Shards of bone and cartilage protruded from its arms, body, and legs. It carried hot coals and moaned terribly as the coals burnt its arms and chest. When the creature reached them, it forced hot coals into Durant's mouth. Durant passed out and the demon turned towards Adel, forcing coals into her mouth. She passed out after the second coal was forced between her lips.

Adel awakened in a cell, still suspended upside down. The three headed creature lay unconscious, or dead, on the ground. Its chest had burned away where it had been holding the coals. The eyes on the middle head opened and stared at her. There was no malice in its expression. If anything, she saw sadness. The eyes closed and she wondered if the brains in the other two heads were dead.

She coughed and three burning coals fell from her mouth. The pain in her throat and mouth made her scream and, this time, it echoed around the confined space. Durant looked lifeless beside her. She remembered what he said about taking a double dose of the serum and wondered if he was dead yet. She realised he couldn't be dead because she was still inside his dream. In a moment of panic, she imagined that he had died, and she was trapped inside his never-ending dream world.

He moaned a moment later, and she cried out in relief.

The respite did not last. A carbonised sharded creature entered the cell. More shadow than anything else, it grabbed hold of Adel by the arms and pulled. It kept pulling until her body ripped away from her legs.

Adel vomited bloody puke but, oddly, she felt no pain. Her head spun as she looked up at her amputated legs. They remained spiked to the metal rod through her ankles.

The sharded flipped her around and hung her by the wrists from a steel hook bolted to the ceiling. Staring at the entrails swaying from her abdomen, a new source of agony rushed through her. Every inch of her intestines coursed with intense pain. She remained suspended that way for what seemed like days. During that time, various sharded would enter the cell and eat part of her entrails. Every bite seared through her whole body like lightning splinters of pain.

When the light began to darken, Adel knew Durant would soon be dead. She had only experienced death once before inside a dream, when a gimp masked host was brutalising her in a Japanese S&M torture house. Right before the climax of his brutal torture show, he had a heart attack.

She knew what to expect from death.

The darkness expanded from the edge of her vision, moving inwards. Slowly at first, like twilight turning into night. The darkness quickened its pace until there was only a small circle of light before her eyes. A tiny pinprick. Total blackness.

She heard shallow breathing.

Not her own breathing, not even Durant's.

Close to her ear.

A voice.

"I like the smell of your liver, Mother-Never-to-Be," it said. *"That means you can avoid this ending. Just remember that when the time comes, and my servant arrives, eat the liver set out before you without raising questions of conscience. When we eventually meet, you can call me Snake and I will call you wife."*

Then, utter silence deafened her into unconsciousness.

Adel awakened with a shock and saw Sykes standing over her.

"Durant is dead," he said.

She didn't need to be told.

"You have to stay for the investigation."

Adel got up from the bed and walked towards Durant. She kissed him on the forehead.

"You deal with the police," she said to Sykes.

"But you need to talk to them. To answer their questions."

Adel walked over to the door, opened it, and closed it behind her. She left the apartment block and made her way to Notre Dame. It was late in the afternoon, and she just made the last admissions. Inside the cathedral, she walked over to the bench she had shared with Durant in his dream and sat down. She focused on the echoing footsteps of the few people still inside and wept. She didn't ever want to leave the cathedral. Three months later, she still had not left.

"You are nearly finished," the nun said to Adel.

"Yes," Adel replied.

"Once you've finished the Old Testament, you can start on the New."

"Yes."

"He will be pleased."

"Perhaps."

"Do you still have the nightmare about your child?"

"No."

"His word has cleansed you."

"No."

"What then?"

"He has simply exchanged one nightmare for another."

The nun sat beside her on the bench. "People are still frightened," she said. "They saw their dead relatives, friends, and past lovers inside Durant's dream. People from all corners of the world saw their dead in the dream. That means it was more than a dream. The people of the world want you to be their dream host again. They want to know more about the hot place. More people have turned towards His word since you revealed the true Hell than at any other time in history. You must show them more. People are calling you a saint."

Adel continued to read the bible as she spoke. "I am no saint and I have no intention of experiencing the hot place ever again."

"What will you do then?"

"I will wait."

"Wait for what?"

"Did you know the ancients thought the liver was the seat of life? The soul. One thing dream sequencing can't reveal is what your soul experiences in dreams. I'm telling you now, my soul is waiting for the time when it can eat the seat of life without raising questions of conscience. When that day arrives, I think all my nightmares will disappear."

Ears

Darlington 2100

The main beams of the Viva illuminated the country road like a black and white tunnel shifting in a dry electric storm. Shady hedgerows and bare-leafed trees flashed by too quickly. Fergus eased off the accelerator. If he hadn't slowed down, his black and white journey would have twisted into red. Pressing down hard on the brakes, the Viva screeched to a dead stop. Fergus's breathing quickened as the adrenaline rush took hold. He gawped at the road ahead. A family of badgers stood immobile in the middle of the road. They waited in line, with the boar at the head, two cubs in the middle, and a sow at the rear. The boar stared back at him, as if it was slightly concerned, but no more than that. Its fur bristled in the car's headlights, while its eyes gleamed intelligence. It raised its head, as if saluting Fergus, acknowledging his braking skills.

Fergus relaxed his grip on the steering wheel.

The cubs began to fidget. The sow nipped the nearest one and it settled them down. As the boar started to move, the rest of the family followed his lead before slipping away into the darkness beyond the bushes at the side of the road.

When they were gone, Fergus thought back to that day at the beach. The sun, low in the sky but still warm, turned everything into silhouette. They walked in line across the flat, sandy beach. Fergus at the head, their two children in the middle, and his wife, Pennie, at the rear. Watching their shadows trace ridiculous steps at their sides, laughter tripped the breeze. He always went back to that day when he felt down. Thinking about the boar at the head of its family, Fergus wondered if he ever felt unhappy; if it had a place inside its mind where it could escape from responsibility.

Twenty minutes later, Fergus pulled the Viva into the small car park that gave no indication of the importance of the building it supported. He waited a few minutes, then reluctantly got out of the car. Although he had worked at Glinka for over three months, today was the first day he would be introduced to *the man*. He had been instructed not to call him by any name until the man told him what he wanted to be called. Everyone received a different name when first introduced. Fergus made his way to the glass entranceway, swiped his security pass across the reader, and waited for the door to open. He entered the reception area. The security guard studied him as he walked by.

"Morning," Fergus said.

As usual, the sullen guard barely nodded his head in response.

At the changing room, Fergus met his supervisor, Patrick Wainwright. They small talked while Fergus removed his clothing and replaced it with sterile area clothing which consisted of latex gloves, a non-shedding boiler suit, a hood that covered all his face apart from his eyes and knee length boots that he fastened around his legs with ties. At each stage of the changing procedure, he sprayed his gloved hands with disinfectant to reduce the bio burden his body naturally produced. Staring at himself in the stainless-steel mirror, he completed the changing procedure by placing the irradiated goggles over his eyes and once more sprayed his gloved hands with the disinfectant.

"You're a natural at this," Wainwright said when he finished.

"You've passed the micro tests without a single bacterial growth count. They don't come any more sterile than Fergus Peterson."

"It's all your training," Fergus said, smiling behind the hooded mask he wore.

"Speaking of training, I know I've said this several times, but it's worth repeating."

"Don't mention the crucifixion, right?"

Wainwright smiled. "Right. And if he mentions it, don't respond. He will only get agitated."

"I guess it's time to go meet him."

"Yes, it is. Good luck Fergus."

Wainwright typed a code into the keypad and the door into the man's chamber opened. Fergus stepped inside and the door immediately closed behind him.

Through the glass partition, Fergus saw the man sitting on a seat in the middle of the dimly lit cell with his head in his hands, staring at the floor. He couldn't see or feel the air flow, but he knew there was a positive pressure cascading from the centre of the room outwards to reduce micro-organism contamination in the man's quarters. The whole facility was designed, and standard operating procedures introduced, to ensure the man remained protected from contamination.

"I can't hear Him speak anymore," the man said.

"Can't hear who speak?"

"God, of course, who else did you think I was talking to?"

"Why can't you hear Him speak?"

The man lowered his hands and raised his head. "Because I cut off my ears," he said.

Fergus stared at where the man's ears should have been. In place of them were two bloody holes. As he continued to look, a different image of the man flashed though his mind. In the image, his head looked like it had exploded from inside but remained frozen in mid explosion. The man's ears were missing, but he had two gaping mouths, each with a full set of teeth. One of his eye sockets was blown away, yet both eyes stared at Fergus like they were pleading to him. A voice sounded in his head.

"Sharded like me."

"I want my ears back," the man said as he stood and walked towards the glass. "Get them for me and sew them back on."

Fergus shook his head to clear it. "Where are they?" he asked, feeling incoherent from the images and sounds the man had put inside his head.

"I flushed them down the toilet," the man said in a matter-of-fact way.

Fergus pressed the panic button on his sleeve. The alarm sounded and lights flashed. Instantly, the door to the viewing room opened and men dressed in sterile gowns rushed in.

"He's cut off his ears," Fergus said.

The men ushered Fergus out of the room and Wainwright took him through the de-gowning procedure before they left the area.

"He is calm now," Wainwright said to Fergus later in the canteen. He held a cigarette lighter. He lit and unlit it several times. "He is asking for you."

"Did they find his ears?" Fergus asked.

"No, they are most likely floating somewhere in the sewage works by now. Maybe the rats have eaten them."

Fergus moved his food around the plate without eating any of it. "Why did he cut them off?"

"He said he was tired of listening to God's bullshit."

"I don't want to see him again."

"You know you don't have a choice."

Fergus rubbed his temples, drank his coffee, and went back to the changing rooms with Wainwright. After changing into the sterile gowns, Fergus made a last attempt to convince Wainwright it was a bad idea for him to see the man again.

"I don't..."

"You signed a contract," Wainwright said. "Your family will suffer if you do not fulfil your obligations."

Fergus knew what he was getting into, but hearing the threat spoken so bluntly for the first time made him flinch.

"Fuck you, Wainwright."

"As long as you fulfil your obligations, you can fuck me any way you'd like."

Fergus turned his back on Wainwright and sprayed his hands with the sterilising agent. Then, he walked over to the doorway as Wainwright typed in the key code. When the door opened, he stepped into the viewing room. The man sat in the centre of his space behind the glass partition. He must have asked for a straitjacket, because he was strapped into one. The top half of his head was bandaged. Two small spots of blood were visible either side of his head where his ears should be. He stared at the floor as Fergus walked up to the glass.

"They couldn't find my ears," the man said.

"No," Fergus said, not wanting to repeat that Wainwright had joked about the man's ears being rat meat in the sewers.

"I'm getting used to not hearing God speak. That's a bad sign."

"Your ears, I mean... you don't actually hear through them. You hear through your eardrums."

The man stood up and charged at the glass partition, striking his body against it. The noise in the close quarters reverberated.

Fergus jumped back, shaken.

The man sat back down on the floor.

"Fuck you. What do you think I am, senile or something? My ears were symbolic. How else do you expect to hear the voice of the Lord other than through vague associations?"

"I don't know, I've never heard God speak before." Fergus's voice wavered, but at least he managed to say something.

"Of course you've heard Him. You've just forgotten, that's all. You've misplaced the words he says to every new-born. Everyone forgets until the end, when it's too late to grasp the significance of His words."

"The end?"

"Jesus, are you senile? I mean death, of course. The end."

"Of course."

The man looked up at Fergus. "You are mocking me. I like that Fergus. I like people who can mock others. There is hope for you yet."

The man stood up again, walked over to the partition, and stared deeply at Fergus.

"You can call me Snake," he said. "No one has ever called me by that name before. At least, not to my face." He pulled against the straps of the straight jacket. "Do you want to fuck me, Fergus? I can bend over for you if you'd like."

Fergus wanted to move away from the window. He wanted to leave the sterile suite altogether. He did neither. "No, I don't want to do that, Mr Snake."

"Oh wow, I love the way you say my name. *Mr Snake*, just like a lover would say it to me. It's just Snake, by the way. I'm no mister."

"Snake," Fergus repeated.

"What is it that you want to fuck?" the man asked, pulling against the straitjacket. "Everyone wants to fuck something. What are your particular tastes?"

Despite the glass between them, it felt like there was no barrier. "Do you really want me to fuck you?" Fergus asked.

The man laughed. He bent his head back and laughed even more. Fergus hated the way the man laughed.

When he stopped laughing, the man sat down on the floor, crossed legged. "I am not who you think I am."

"Who do you think I think you are?"

The man stood and turned away from Fergus. "Fuck, I so wanna start a zombie holocaust."

"Why would you want to do that, Snake?"

The man looked back at Fergus over his shoulder. "I don't like the way you say my name. Are you God in disguise?"

"Yes."

"Fuck you."

Fergus could feel himself sweat beneath the sterile area clothing. "Why are you here? Why am *I* here?"

"I'm here because I wanted to feel what it was like to be human. Yet, once I became a man, my spirit weakened this feeble human body it now resides within. Worse still, being close to humans is like a cancer to me in this form. I come out in spots and vomit all over the place just by being close to another person. Now that I am man, I still cannot experience what it is like to be man. How perverse. Just like it was before. I still need to keep my distance from you creatures, but for a different reason."

"You never answered why I am here."

"You need the money, Fergus." The man sat down on the metal seat at the far wall of his cell. He started to squirm, like he was attempting to worm his way out of the straitjacket.

"I want to leave this place. I've been here too long. Remove your sterile clothing. I want to see how you look semi-naked. And open the door. I'm getting out of this place, pronto."

"If I do what you ask, you will die."

The man bent down and wiped his mouth on his shoulder. "This body I'm trapped in will die, I won't. What's the point of living just to be a prisoner?"

Fergus hesitated. He didn't want to open the door. Not because he didn't want the man's body to die, he didn't want to open the door because he didn't want to get any closer to the man. He took off the sterile boots anyway, then the gown, the mask and lastly, the hood.

He stood there in his underpants and socks.

He opened the door.

"How did you keep isolated two thousand years ago?" Fergus asked.

"I didn't need protection from humanity then. It's only been in the last fifty years that man started to contaminate me. Maybe it's God's way of showing me I'm too old to carry on living amongst humans."

The man stood up and walked through the doorway towards the exit. He looked at the camera above the door. "Open up," he said.

Fergus heard a click and the door swung open.

"Do you want me to remove the straitjacket?" Fergus asked.

"No," the man said, as he stepped into the changing room. "My jacket keeps me out of trouble. It stops me from doing things without thinking them through properly. If all of humanity were strapped into straightjackets, the world would be much more equal and fairer, but how God-damned boring it would be."

Fergus followed the man and, once inside, the door behind him closed. Wainwright stood opposite, staring at the man. He had never seen anyone look so anxious.

"Take me to the lab, Mr Wainwright," the man said. "I want my ears back."

"Your ears are somewhere in the drainage system," Fergus said, as he put his clothes back on. "You flushed them down the toilet."

"My ears are in the lab," the man said. "Everything I flush down that minging toilet goes to the lab for analysis."

"Of course, Fat Controller," Wainwright said. "Please, follow me."

Fergus was not surprised Wainwright had lied to him, just disappointed. "He makes you call him, Fat Controller?" he asked Wainwright.

"I make him call me that," the man said, "and I make him get down on his knees and say his prayers to me before he goes to bed at night."

They followed Wainwright out of the changing room, along a seemingly endless white corridor, past a few doorways until he stopped at a stainless-steel door with a small glass window. Wainwright peered through the window, then opened the door, and they entered the lab. The four lab technicians inside stared at the man, then turned away from him and went about their business with their heads down.

The man's ears were beneath a bell jar on one of the lab benches. They were held in place by several pins, as if someone had stretched the ears to make them appear larger.

"Pick up my ears, Mr Wainwright," the man said.

Wainwright raised the bell jar, removed the pins and picked up the ears. Holding them in his outstretched hand, he offered both ears to the man.

The man stared at them for a short while. "Put them in your pocket," he said. "Take us to the restaurant."

"Why the restaurant?" Fergus asked, picking up a scalpel from the bench and putting it in his pocket without anyone seeing.

"I want to see Mr Wainwright eat my ears and I don't expect him to do that without a clean plate and cutlery. Then there are condiments. A man cannot be expected to eat another man's ears without a touch of seasoning."

It wasn't until they reached the restaurant that the man began to cough. Staring at him, Fergus noticed his pale skin was becoming red and blotchy.

"What, you've never seen anyone die before?" the man said after he stopped coughing. "Don't you realise everyone is dying? From the very first moment you are conceived, Fergus, you are dying. Don't fret, though. It feels enlivening at the end. Being close to death is like nothing else you will experience. Not even reincarnation is as memorable as death."

Fergus didn't know how to respond, so he said nothing. As soon as they entered the restaurant, and the other diners saw the man, the only sound was knives and forks against plates.

They sat together at a table by the window. A half-dead tulip drooped in a vase in the centre of the table. Wainwright left them while he went to get a clean plate, a knife, a fork, and salt and pepper. When he returned, he sat opposite the man and placed the ears on the white plate. He sprinkled salt and pepper on each ear and then tentatively sliced into one with the knife, before mechanically lifting it to his mouth and pulling it from the fork with his teeth. He chewed on the ear without any emotion in his face.

"Why are you making him do this?" Fergus asked.

"I'm not making him do anything; he has free will."

"He wouldn't eat your ears if he didn't feel threatened. Everyone in this restaurant feels the same way. It has something to do with you."

The man stared at Fergus, taking his eyes away from Wainwright for the first time since he started eating the ears. "Do you feel threatened, Fergus?"

Fergus thought for a moment before answering. "Not threatened, more not in control."

"You can leave any time you want."

"Really?"

"Yes, really."

Fergus stood up.

The man watched Wainwright eat again. "Of course, for every action, there is a consequence."

An image flashed through Fergus's mind. In the image, half of a woman's face exploded outwards in a frozen gristly blast with her right eye disconnected from its socket, yet still, it remained connected to her.

"Sharded like me."

Fergus sat back down.

"Are you sure you're not hungry?" the man asked Fergus.

Fergus shook his head.

"You could have some liver and chips. You know the hepar is the centre of the soul. Only something that smells as sweet as the hepar can be considered the centre of the soul. You should eat more liver and become truly connected to your inner self."

When Wainwright finished eating, he pulled the tulip out of the vase, and gulped down the water from the vase.

"What did my ears taste like?" the man asked.

"Good," Wainwright replied.

"Don't lie to me."

"They were like the gristle you normally don't eat on meat. They tasted how I'd expect an uncooked sheep's brain to taste."

"And you still ate them. You need to grow some balls man. Learn how to say no to the bully. Hell, if I thought you had any balls, I'd cut them off right now and watch Fergus eat them with a plateful of fries."

No one spoke for a while until the man stood up. "Fine company you two make for the end of days," he said. "Let's go see if we can find some other entertainment to keep us interested in life."

They left the restaurant and made their way to the main exit. At the reception area, the man walked over to the security guard.

"I know you are carrying a handgun. It's a revolver, right?"

The security guard remained glum and silent.

"Revolvers are amazingly robust, more so than automatic pistols. There are too many working parts to an automatic pistol, too many things to go wrong. A revolver is beautifully simple. You can stick a revolver in a steel box, put it in a hole and leave it there until you feel threatened. Dig it up fifty years later, clean it, load it with fresh bullets, and presto, it is ready to shoot. You feel threatened now, correct, Stewart?"

Stewart nodded.

"You are right to feel threatened. Everything is about to change. Do yourself a favour. Take that revolver out of your ankle holster, put it in your mouth, and press the trigger. Make sure you aim the barrel into the roof of your mouth, not the back of your throat. How many times have suicides blown a hole through their mouths and not killed themselves? I'll tell you, too many times."

"Please, don't make him do it," Fergus said to the man.

The man ignored Fergus and continued to talk to the security guard. "It would be an awful shame if you wasted your father's thoughtful gesture. He knew you'd need the gun one day. Well, that day is here."

The security guard bent down and raised his trousers. He pulled the gun from the holster. He aimed it at the man.

"Fuck," the man said. "That's what I hate about my influence. It's so fucking unpredictable."

The security guard pressed the trigger.

Click.

The man shook his head. "You numb fuck," he said. "You forgot to load the gun, didn't you? For every action, there is a consequence. I won't forget this action when the day of reckoning comes, Stewart."

Heading for the exit, Wainwright opened the door for the man and Fergus followed them outside into the dark night. As they crossed the road to the car park, Fergus heard a loud bang behind. He turned around and saw the security guard slumped back against his chair. Red specks of blood and brain were splattered against the glass partition all around him.

"Looks like he took my advice," the man said. "He aimed for the roof of his mouth. Anyway, forget Stewart. I want a drink. Take me to a bar, Fergus."

They got into the car. The man sat in the passenger seat while Wainwright got in the rear. Fergus attempted to fasten the man's seatbelt, but the man nudged him away.

"I don't need a seatbelt, Fergus. I've got a straitjacket to keep me strapped in."

Fergus gunned the engine and pulled out of the car park. "It's three in the morning. All the bars are closed," he said.

"I know the owner of a nice little town centre bar. He will open it up for me. Ring this number," he said to Wainwright, reciting the telephone number from memory.

Wainwright did as he said and when he got an answer, he held the phone against the side of the man's face.

"Yes, I know how late it is," the man said. "No, you don't know me. I know about Saul, though. I know all about Saul and what the others did to him. What do I want? I want a drink. I want you to open your bar and serve me your finest vodka."

The man pushed aside the phone with his head when he was finished speaking and Wainwright put his phone back in his pocket.

"It's done," the man said. "Now take me to Bar None and make it quick. We don't have much time."

Fergus barely heard his words as he stared at the road up ahead and saw the two young badgers and the sow. They were in a line. The two cubs close to the road verge and the sow directly behind them. All three were flattened red against the tarmac.

"Oh," the man said as they drove past the dead family. "That would be my influence."

Fergus thought about the boar, wondering how its mind would process the loss of its family. What was it thinking now? What was it doing now?

"What would you do?" the man asked.

"What?" Fergus said.

"In the same circumstances as the boar, what would you do?"

"I would kill for my family."

"But who would you kill? The driver or the influence behind his deeds?"

"I would kill everyone."

"Good answer. I always knew you would make a great father one day."

They reached Bar None a while later and Fergus parked the car across the road from it. He got out and saw that Wainwright was slumped, unable to move. Walking over to the rear passenger door, he opened it and helped him out of the car. With Fergus supporting Wainwright, they crossed the road. The bar owner was already waiting for them in the entrance lobby. He unlocked the door and they entered with Fergus still holding onto Wainwright. The man sat at a table near the window while the owner busied himself switching on the lights where they sat.

"Bring a full bottle of vodka," the man said to the owner. "Not that cheap stuff on the back shelf either. I want the French vodka you keep under the counter. The high alcohol content stuff you feed Saul. Bring ice and lime too."

Fergus and Wainwright sat at the man's table and, a moment later, the owner placed a tray on the table with two bottles of premium vodka, three glasses, a bucket of ice, a bowl of limes, and a knife.

"Leave us," the man said.

The owner walked across to the exit and gently closed the door behind him as he left.

"Can you see him changing?" the man said to Fergus.

Fergus stared at Wainwright. "Yes. What have you done to him?"

"Fix our drinks and I will tell you."

Fergus took the knife and sliced three thin strips of lime. He put one piece of lime and one ice cube into each glass.

Using his teeth, the man placed an extra slice of lime in their drinks. "Forgive my teeth but I like to help, even if it is only a little."

Fergus opened the bottle and poured vodka into each glass until it covered the ice and lime.

"I like the way you fix drinks," the man said.

Fergus held one of the glasses up to the man's lips and he took a sip.

"Excellent," the man said.

Fergus sipped his drink, and something caught in his throat. Probably a piece of lime, he thought. He gulped back the remainder of his vodka in one go and poured himself another, without replacing the lime.

Wainwright's eyes were closed. His head was slumped forwards.

"You were going to tell me what you've done to him," Fergus said.

"You don't think he could eat my flesh without consequences, do you? Even though I am currently in the form of a man, my influence remains sublime."

"Your flesh has poisoned him?"

"In a way, yes, he is infected."

"To what end?"

The man clicked his tongue on the roof of his mouth, "We need a new kind of cancer," he said. "It might not seem so to you right now, but you guys are winning the battle against cancer. In a few more decades, you will discover an awesome new medicine and cancer, as you know it, will pretty much seem like a common flu infection."

Another image flashed through Fergus's mind. This time it wasn't the man he saw; this time he saw himself. His head was deformed and oversized. Splinters of gristle grew out of the top and sides of his head, and partially covered his eyes and nose. From a slash in his chest, blood pumped and rose in an arc before it fell into his gaping mouth.

"Why do you keep showing me the images? Are they visions of the future or snapshots of where you come from?"

"It's not me, Fergus. You must be gifted. A favourite child of God who He shares special moments with."

"I've seen your face. I've seen my face. Only, they were different."

"Everything is distorted in His multiple worlds. Even here, what you see is twisted reality. Eyes are not the mirrors of the soul. They are the hoodwinks of His creations."

Fergus fixed them both a fresh drink, thinking on the man's words. "When did you become so fucked up?" he said, as he offered the drink to the man.

The man smiled. "I guess that would be when God lost faith in me. Yeah, I'm pretty sure it was around that time."

"Why did you lose faith in God?"

"I said *He* lost faith in *me*." The man paused. "Fuck, Fergus, you are a sharp one. I see what you are doing. It doesn't matter; I also see you don't want to know the truth. You are just like the rest. And here I was thinking you would make a good father."

The man coughed and vomited on the bar floor. The air was filled with the odour of his puke mixed with vodka, and something else just as rancid. Despite not wanting to, Fergus found himself breathing in the stench. He covered his nose and mouth with his hand and said, "I want to know where I fit into your plans."

"I feel lousy," the man said. "Being human is not all it's made out to be. I can't wait to die and get out of this feeble body."

"How long have you been a man?"

"I know you already know the answer to that question. They must have told you about my origins."

The man lowered his head a little and Fergus thought he detected something like sadness cross his face. "I could not believe it when I saw Him on the cross. I had never experienced so much pain in the world as I did that day. I wanted to run. I wanted to hide. I wanted to destroy the world and every human in it. In the end, I fell asleep. When I awakened a few weeks ago, I absorbed the man you see before you."

"You just decided to possess a random man in the crowd?"

"It's a cheap trick, I know, but I did not have the means to be conceived by parents then. A birth is far superior to seizing another's body, but we must work with what we have until we have something more."

Wainwright toppled forwards and his head banged against the table. Fergus lifted him up and pushed him back into his seat. He checked for a pulse but couldn't find one.

"He's dead," Fergus said.

"In a way," the man said.

"What do you mean?"

"The dead have a way of coming back to life. Haven't you watched TV or movies recently? Everywhere you look the dead are walking. Don't you know that almost everything humanity can imagine, they can create?"

"What kind of cancer have you created?"

"Don't act dumb. You know what kind it is."

"Fuck," Fergus said, standing up and backing away from the table. "This is the start of the holocaust you were talking about."

"Isn't it a blast? A holocaust started after a man eats my ears. Who the fuck could have come up with a masterpiece like that, other than me?"

"How does the infection spread?"

"Not by ear wax, that's for sure. Maybe blood, maybe saliva, maybe both. It could be an airborne thing, I honestly don't know yet. I never was any good at the scientific side of things. I am more your creative type."

Wainwright raised his head from the table and slowly opened his eyes.

The man had another coughing fit. "Can you imagine it, a boar and a sow going through the anguish of losing a cub, only for that cub to be resurrected moments after its death? How elated they would feel. It wouldn't last, of course. Not when the cub wants to eat its parents. Well, eat the tastiest part of them I mean. Look at Wainwright. Watch how rapidly his flesh transforms into so much more, a sharded thing of beauty. I wonder how his brain will transform. How much he will keep, how much he will lose, what he will gain. One thing is for sure, he will have an appetite. His soul remains, of course, but it is suffering. Imagine that, can you Fergus? A true suffering soul of a psychopath unleashed on the world. Creating a new life form is so rewarding. I should have done it an age ago."

Fergus stared at Wainwright. Something moved beneath the surface of his skin. Shards of bone, cartilage, or some other substance grew out of his forehead and continued around the top half of his skull until it looked like he wore a crown of thorns. His nose twisted, then split in two and covered his eyes. A loud crack sounded in the bar, as Wainwright's lower jaw snapped in half and doubled in size. Sharded teeth sprouted from his mouth like fragments of broken glass. Throughout the process, Wainwright remained perfectly still.

Fergus backed away as the transformation continued.

"Do not worry," the man said, "he will not bite you. He is not a flesh eater, yet. I'm not even sure if he will ever become a flesh eater. That's just something the movies make up, right? Oops, I almost forgot my own supposition. Whatever humanity can imagine, humanity can create."

"What about you? What happens when you die, Snake?"

"What do you mean?"

"Won't you be trapped inside the man's body you possessed when it dies? If it's infected with this new cancer, it won't actually be dead. I mean, you have been in close contact with Wainwright, what makes you think he hasn't infected you already?"

The man got up from his chair and made a move to the exit.

"Where are you going?" Fergus asked.

"To die in peace."

"You aren't infected yet, are you? Wainwright isn't contagious yet."

At the door, the man attempted to open it. Unable to turn the knob, he gave up. "Open this for me," he told Fergus.

"No."

The man turned around and stared at Fergus. "What do you mean, no?"

"I don't want to open the door. I want you to stay here. I want you to experience what it feels like for a man to turn into a zombie."

"Not a zombie, a sharded. Humans created zombies. I created the sharded."

"You've only created one, so far. If I kill Wainwright, then you won't create any more."

"You have balls, Fergus. I'll give you that. Now open the door for me before I get angry."

"How long will it take for Wainwright to become contagious?"

"I already told you; I don't know how long. I don't even know how the infection will spread. All I know for sure is that eating my flesh is enough to start the process."

"But you don't want to take the chance of becoming infected by staying here with him."

Wainwright rocked back and forth. He moaned softly as if trying to speak, but no words came from him. His tongue suddenly protruded out of his mouth. It looked twice the size it should be, and it licked the air, searching for something Fergus could not imagine. More slivers of bone grew from him, this time coming from his neck and growing past his ears. He shook his head from side to side as a splinter jutted out from where his left eye should have been, and he screamed wildly. Wainwright looked like the images the man had put into Fergus's mind earlier.

"Sharded like me."

"If we don't leave soon, we will both be infected," the man said.

"Even if we leave, I will be infected eventually, but you will die before the contagion spreads quickly enough to reach you. Is that your plan?"

"What if it is?"

"You are in a straitjacket. You are weak. I think I'll keep you here with Wainwright until you die. When you become sharded, you'll be trapped inside your current body. Maybe trapped for another two thousand years."

"Who are you Fergus? Are you one of His new angels? One I have never met?"

"I'm just a man. A man with a family I will do anything to

protect."

"I think you are wrong. I can smell the darkness inside your liver. You have hidden the truth from yourself for far too long."

Fergus stared at Wainwright. He grabbed the bottle of vodka they drank from and poured it over Wainwright. He didn't smoke, but Fergus knew Wainwright had a lighter in his pocket that he lit and unlit whenever he was nervous.

"This is a mistake, Fergus," the man said. "You will change the course of history if you do this. Don't you know humanity is a scourge? It will destroy the planet and everything on it if it isn't stopped."

Fergus warily bent into Wainwright and got the lighter from his pocket. He lit it and placed the flame against Wainwright. The sleeve of his coat started to burn and when the vodka took hold of the flame it *whooshed* into life.

Fergus put the unopened bottle of vodka in his pocket and backed away from Wainwright.

"We should get out of here, Fergus," the man said.

"You don't want to die in these flames?" Fergus said. "I thought you'd be at home burning alive."

The man shrugged. "Whatever."

Fergus walked towards the door and twisted the knob. He exited the bar with the man close behind. Standing in the middle of the road, he watched Wainwright burn inside the bar. He did not scream or move and that somehow made it worse.

"I should call the fire brigade," he said.

The man stood beside him, watching the spectacle unfold inside the bar. "You've already ruined my sharded holocaust. At least let me enjoy a good burning."

Without warning, Wainwright stood up and his burning body ran towards the large bar window. He didn't stop running when he reached it. He burst through in a shower of glass and landed face down on the ground. His still burning body twitched for a while until there was no movement at all.

"The end," the man said. "It was more like a pilot episode than a full-blown movie."

Fergus called the fire brigade on his mobile and reported the fire.

"Take me to Blackwell Path," the man said. "I want to die near a river."

They got into Fergus' car and pulled away from the kerb. The man remained silent during the drive. Glancing over at him from time to time, Fergus saw saliva drooling from his mouth and the blotches on his face were more pronounced. He stopped the car at the roadside by Blackwell Path and helped the man out of the car. Supporting the man, they walked along the path until they came to the riverbank where the man slumped down.

Fergus sat beside him, exhausted.

It was a while before the man spoke. "Dying like a man is beautiful," he said in a serene voice.

"What makes it beautiful?" Fergus asked.

Daybreak formed in the sky and Fergus thought about being home, in bed with his wife. The body heat he felt when he first got into bed each morning and hugged Pennie after finishing night shift was one of his favourite experiences. He stared at his hand. Something moved beneath his skin like there was an insect underneath it.

"It's the way it makes you think differently about all the things that have ever happened in your life," the man murmured. "There is so much clarity. So much understanding of the things that are important and the things that are just noise."

"What are you thinking about now?"

"Flying through the Xibalba Nebula, circling a death star, with a seraph I used to call a friend at my side. Afterwards, our wings glistened with morning dew as we rested in the treetops of a nameless rainforest waiting for two suns to rise. I could taste the wind in those days like I can taste a good wine these days. Trust me Fergus, you need to die soon. You need to see things differently, like I see things now."

The man fell backwards and lay on the grass staring at the sky.

"What do you see now?" Fergus said.

The man closed his eyes. "I see myself biting off the tip of my tongue and spitting it into your vodka."

"You've known all along the infection can only be spread by eating infected flesh."

Fergus didn't need him to answer.

A short while later the man stopped breathing.

Fergus pulled the bottle from his pocket and opened it. He took a long swig of the vodka. He didn't know what to say to Pennie. He could not explain what happened over a text. He did not have time to speak on the phone. He would not be able to do what he must if he heard Pennie speak. There was only one thing he could do.

I love you, wife, he texted. *I have always loved you and always will.*

He drank more vodka and waited until the one sun in the partially cloudy sky appeared on the horizon. Removing the scalpel from his pocket, he placed the blade against his skin. His hand trembled. How did anyone find the strength to cut their own skin? He remembered the cubs, how the man had said their death was his influence.

Lou and Joe.

His cubs.

He made a single cut, then cut his other wrist.

Blood rapidly covered his hands and dripped onto the grass.

He poured the remainder of the vodka over the man and himself, then lay back on the dry grass. It would burn well. He could not set them alight until he had lost enough blood so that he would pass out before the agony of the flames took hold. It was a fine balance, and he hoped he would not lose consciousness before he started the blaze. It was vital that he sterilised the contagion.

When Fergus started to feel drowsy with the loss of blood, he pressed the lighter button.

Nothing.

He pressed it several times.

Still nothing.

Wainwright must have been more nervous than usual in the night.

Consequences.

Waves of blackness pulsed through him. Close to death, Fergus thought about Pennie's body heat in the morning. Her warmth comforted him. It comforted him until the final dark wave washed everything away. And then, light flashed across his eyes. Immense pain pulsed through his body. His head creaked and groaned as his skull found a different shape. His right eye expanded and contracted as a shard forced it out of his eye socket until his eye stood out from his face like a tentacle on a slug. He wanted to scream as the bones in his jaw snapped and cracked themselves into a new shape, transforming his mouth into a gaping orifice that he could not fully close. His teeth were forced out of his gums and replaced by the shards that pushed them out.

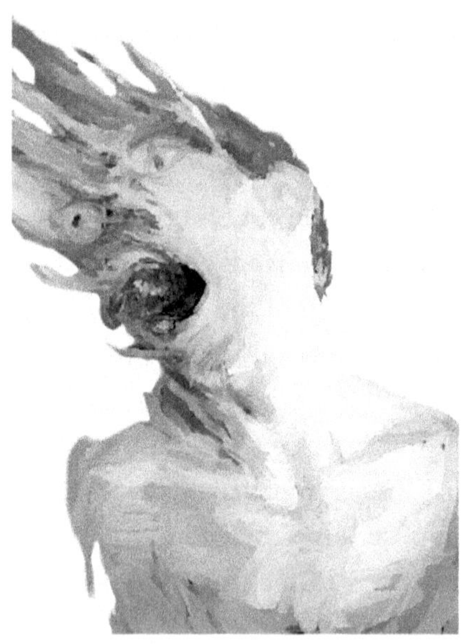

Once the mutation ceased, Fergus held his hands up to his head and felt the shard cartilage and bone pointing out from his face. He should have been horrified, but he was not. A voice spoke to him inside his head; a voice he recognised.

"Follow the scent."

As soon as the words formed in his mind, Fergus could smell the sweetest fragrance of all. It came from every direction. An unbearable need to get up and follow wherever the scent led him coursed through his being. He looked down at the body below. The scent came from it too, but it smelled different. It didn't make him want to feed.

He stood up and followed the path leading up to... he could not remember where the path led. It did not matter. All that mattered was the scent. Finding its source and then...

"Then it is time to eat," the voice said. *"Eat the centre of another's soul and feed it to your own soul."*

Yes, Fergus thought, *eat*.

"Then you must hurry and find Izabella, and in turn, she must bear you a child."

Iz

Texas 2100

Sitting around the fire listening to them talk reminded Iz of the night Adam died. She didn't know why she was there. She didn't belong with this group of people. Unable to share her life with strangers, with anyone, she accepted a dare rather than tell a truth.

"No one has ever been inside," Peyton said. "Your dare is to break into the church and take a picture with your phone."

"Take a picture of what?" Iz asked.

"A picture of you pissing in the font."

Some of them in the circle laughed; some of them looked dismayed. Iz got up and walked away from them, heading for the church.

It was a well-cared for church. The grounds and outside fabric of the building were maintained by a local contractor who claimed he didn't deal directly with anyone connected to the church. He was paid by an upstate agent. No one in town had ever been inside the church and no one had ever seen anyone leave or enter it either. There were no signs or symbols indicating which religion the church belonged to. It had always been there, and everyone had always accepted that it was a church.

Iz opened the gate and walked along the path leading to the church entrance. At the doorway she twisted the handle, expecting the door to be locked. It wasn't and when she pushed, it swung inwards. The doorway led to a small antechamber with stone walls and flooring. It was empty of furnishings, other than a plain wooden bench placed against the left-hand wall, and a light fitting hanging from the arched ceiling. A door, similar in shape but smaller in size to the main entrance, stood directly opposite.

Iz stepped into the antechamber. As soon as she was inside, the door behind her closed and the light went out. She didn't panic. She never panicked, not even when she dropped Adam on his head and heard his neck break. She pulled her phone out of her jeans and used the light from it to get her bearings. She checked the door she just came through. It was locked. She sat on the bench. There was no signal on her phone. Staring at the other door, she had a feeling it would be unlocked, but she didn't want to open it just yet.

Something dropped from the ceiling. Iz turned the phone around, illuminating the space. The glass light shade lay unbroken on the floor. She bent down for a closer look. A bloodied incisor tooth poked out of the shade's metal fastening. Something else dropped from the ceiling. Iz moved the light across the floor and saw another tooth. She felt something hit her head. It dropped onto her shoulder, then onto the floor. It was a molar. She picked up the tooth and studied it. It was a good tooth, no dentist filling required. She wondered if it belonged to a child. No, it was too big to belong to a child. It belonged to someone who looked after their teeth. She put the tooth in her pocket, stood up, and walked over to the door opposite the entrance. It was unlocked.

She stepped through the doorway and found herself in a room twice the size of the antechamber. The only light in the room came from a fire burning inside a metal basket in the centre of the space. The walls looked like they were burning as light from the fire flickered on them. Gazing around, she saw that, just like the antechamber, there were two doors in this room; the one she had come through, and a door directly opposite. She walked over to the fire and warmed herself by the flames.

The door behind her closed.

She checked her phone. There was still no signal. She looked at the door she came through, convinced it would be locked. She walked over to the door anyway and twisted the handle. It was locked. The fire started to spit embers and one of them landed on her arm. It smouldered through the sleeve of her jacket and burned her skin. She quickly took off her jacket and brushed away the still burning ember. Another ember hit her trainer and quickly burned through the leather. She kicked the ember off and ran over to the other door as more embers flew across the room.

The doorway opened into a narrow stairway leading upwards. She put her coat back on and climbed the stairs. The door behind her closed. As she ascended the stairs, the passageway became more and more narrow, until her shoulders touched both walls on either side of her. Further, she had to stoop down as the ceiling began to lower until eventually, she had to crawl on her hands and knees up the stairs.

In the dimly lit stairway, the outline of a door appeared up ahead. It was no more than a fifteen-inch square. She did not think she was small enough to reach it. Even with her arms outstretched in front of her, she could barely crawl in the ever-contracting space. She could not turn back, flames rose behind. The heat in the confined space rapidly increased. It felt like the heat made her body expand in the staircase. Iz forced herself towards the door until she could no longer move or breathe. Her fingers were inches away from the door. Sweat trickled down her forehead and stung her right eye. Her body convulsed as it attempted to fill her lungs with air, but only her arms and legs moved in the cramped space. Her vision went black. She felt like she was falling. Somewhere inside her mind, she heard the door open.

A blast of cold air hit her face. Someone grabbed her hands and pulled her further into the cramped space. It felt like her arms were going to be ripped from her shoulders. She opened her eyes and saw the hunched silhouette of a man in the open doorway. He had one of his feet against the wall as he pulled harder, until her arms and head shot through the opening. With the combined effort of Iz pushing with her feet against the wall and the man pulling her, she finally sprawled out of the opening onto the floor. The cold stone against her face felt uplifting.

Iz lay still on the floor, just breathing. A moment later, she sat up and looked around to see who had pulled her through the doorway. A man sat behind her with his arms and legs crossed. His chin rested on his knees as he stared back at her. She recognised the man. It was Gilbert Spencer.

He died over a month ago.

"Mr Spencer," Iz said.

"You know me?" Spencer asked.

"You used to live across the street from me."

"I've never seen you before in my life."

Iz wondered if he knew he was dead but didn't want to ask him. More so, she wondered if she was dead too. It seemed the only explanation for her being there with him.

"Where are we?" Iz said.

"I was hoping you could answer that."

"The building I entered was a church. I'm not so sure I'm inside a church now, though. How did you get here?"

"I... Someone was chasing me. I was outside. I don't know how I got in here."

"Who was chasing you?"

"A detachment of SS stormtroopers. They had dogs. And... their faces were... They had spikes coming out of their faces, like the ones in that priest's dream."

"What priest?"

"The only priest. The one in Paris who shared his dream with the world."

"Where are they now?"

"I don't know. I lost them when... I don't know when I lost them."

Iz looked around the room. It was similar in size and shape to the room with the fire. There was a normal sized door opposite the small one she had just come through. She stood up and walked over to the larger door.

"What are you doing?" Spencer said.

"Trying to find a way out," Iz answered as she twisted the handle and pulled the door open.

She couldn't see anything inside the next room. It was like the air was painted black. She took her phone from her pocket and turned on the torch application. The light from the phone barely penetrated the space, like the dark was eating the light. She stepped into the room and Spencer followed close behind. As she walked further into the room, the door behind closed and it became even darker. Iz no longer had a reference point to use as a guide to lead her to the door. She could see no more than a few inches in front of her. She knew there would be another door directly opposite the one she came in. Slowly, she walked across the room heading in the direction she hoped the door would be in.

"Where are you?" Spencer asked with a tremor in his voice.

"I'm here. I'm sure there's another door. I'm trying to find it."

"I can't see you. I can't see anything."

"Why did you pull me from the stairway? What made you open the door?"

"I heard you knocking. When I saw your hand, I just grabbed it and pulled."

Iz couldn't remember knocking on the door. She was pleased Spencer had rescued her anyway. She could only help him if she could find the door and open it. She carefully continued forward. It felt like she had been walking for ages, yet she still hadn't reached the other side of the room. She felt Spencer's hand on her shoulder. Despite her surprise, she didn't flinch. She thought about how he died. A gang of vigilantes said Spencer was a snitch. They chased him into an alleyway and beat him to death. His head had been stamped on so badly that it was as flat as a sheet of paper. Iz was disappointed when she checked the alleyway after the ambulance took him away. There was hardly any blood on the ground. She wanted to see lots of Spencer's blood covering the ground.

Spencer stumbled and his hand left her shoulder.

"Where are you?" he said.

His voice sounded distant.

"Over here. Can't you see the light from my phone?"

Dog barks echoed in the distance.

"They are coming for me again!"

The barking got louder, like it came from inside the room now. Iz heard men shouting in German accents. Then a gunshot. Another gunshot. Muzzle flashes revealed glimpses of men and dogs running towards her in the blackness. Spencer screamed. The dogs continued to bark and snarl.

"Get the fuck off me!" Spencer yelled.

It sounded like the dogs were ripping him apart.

Iz listened to the carnage for a while longer then carried on moving forward. She felt the wall against her hand. She moved first left, then right until she felt the outline of the door. She grabbed the handle, twisted, and opened the door. There was a man in the centre of the room, sitting on a wooden bench bolted to the floor. His hands were tied behind his back. He was bare chested but had braces attached to his trousers. His head was slumped forwards. It was covered with a hessian sack that was partially soaked in blood. A placard hanging from a cord around his neck read – *I can't talk anymore.*

Spencer stopped screaming.

Squelching sounds.

Iz turned around.

A searchlight flashed around the room, revealing pockets of activity before it was hidden again when the light moved on and revealed other things.

Two Bullmastiffs were chewing Spencer's face.

They stopped eating, as if they could feel Iz staring at them, and turned towards her. At the same time, several SS troops came into view behind the dogs. Shards of bone and cartilage grew out of their heads, shoulders, and arms. It was their eyes that were the most striking feature. They glowed like eyes caught in a night vision camera and never blinked once.

The searchlight moved and they disappeared into the shadows.

The click of the dog's claws sounded against the stone floor as they slowly moved towards Iz. She continued to watch them as she pulled the door inwards, but it did not move. She pulled again, harder this time, and the door moved a few inches. The dogs started to run, and the troops followed close behind. Iz pulled with all her strength and the door moved further, but still did not fully close. She continued pulling until there was only a two-inch gap between the door and the frame. The Bullmastiffs reached her first and jumped against the door. Their weight, combined with Iz's exertions was enough to force the door shut.

"Dumb dogs," Iz said.

The dogs barked and scratched at the door. A moment later, the noise was joined with shouting in German and bangs against the door. The handle was twisted, but the door did not open. Iz stared at it anyway, expecting it to open at any moment, but it remained closed, and the noise waned.

Then, silence.

Iz shrugged and walked over to the man sitting on the bench. Standing in front of him, she heard a clicking noise. At first, she thought it was the dogs again and turned back towards the door. The sound was too synchronous for dog's claws against stone. After a moment she realised it was a clock ticking. She looked around the room but could not see one anywhere.

To the right of the man was a mobile chest with various bloodied tools on top of it. Next to the tools was an unopened bottle of water. She picked up the water and took a drink. She smelled urine. She checked the bottle. It was the man who smelled of urine. Iz put the bottle down and pulled the sack off his head.

Spencer.

His bottom jaw had been removed. His tongue hung loose like a dog panting for water on a hot day. Iz stared at him, taking in every detail. She shook his shoulder. There was no response. She tried to find a pulse but couldn't. His jaw lay on the floor beneath the seat. She bent down and picked it up. Turning it around in her hands, she saw that some teeth were missing. Maybe the teeth that dropped on her in the antechamber were the ones missing from the jaw. She pulled the tooth out of her pocket and placed it in one of the spaces in the jawbone. It fit perfectly. Looking back at Spencer, she saw that his top set of teeth were still in place. *How had the jaw been removed?* Judging by the jagged flesh, she guessed the jaw had been pulled off rather than sawn off. Removing Spencer's shoelaces, she used them to tie his lower jaw to his upper jaw.

Iz wiped the blood from her hands on the sack and studied her handiwork. Spencer looked more like Spencer, that was a result. Maybe she should take a photo of him. She checked her phone. There was no signal. She did not take a photo.

The sound of barking resumed behind the door.

She moved over to the other door and opened it. A man sat hunched in the corner with his back to her. He was eating something. She stepped into the room.

"Hello," she said.

The man did not answer.

She walked over to him, and the door closed behind her. When she reached the man, she saw that it was Spencer. A different kind of Spencer. This Spencer had two mouths, side by side. He also had two noses. One nose in the normal place on his face, the other beside his right eye.

He was eating an arm. The arm was still attached to a woman lying on the floor. The woman was still alive.

"She cannot feel anything," Spencer said. "She is pumped up with neuro-blockers. It paralyses the senses. Do you want to eat her other arm?"

"What does she taste like?" Iz asked.

"She tastes of fresh blood."

There was a lot of blood on the floor beneath the woman's arm. Iz liked the way the light glinted on the deep red of the blood. "I'm not hungry, maybe later."

"If you step through the door, there will not be a later."

"Why are you eating her arm?"

Spencer turned towards Iz. "You think I should eat her liver instead?"

"I'm not sure. Why would you eat her liver instead of her arm?"

Spencer started eating again. "Maybe you are not what the church thought you could become."

Iz kicked the Spencer in the ribs. "Who is the woman?" she asked.

"She is someone who got trapped in a stairway. Someone who isn't what the church thought she could become."

"How do I get out of the church?"

"Through a door."

Iz stared at Spencer eating for a while longer. She noted how he ate everything to the bone and then licked the bone clean, as if he wanted the woman's skeleton perfectly revealed, and perfectly clean. She wanted to stay to see the woman's skeleton arm fully revealed. She would have preferred to see Spencer's skeleton arm.

Iz kicked Spencer in the ribs until he stopped eating the woman's arm.

"When the drug has worn off, let her eat your arm. Do you understand?"

"Yes".

Iz turned away from Spencer, opened the door, and stepped into the next room.

"Do not tell on me," Spencer yelled.

As soon as the door closed behind her, the noise started. Engines pounded, birds shrieked, and brass instruments playing out of tune infested her head. More sounds joined the pandemonium and Iz clamped her hands over her ears as she staggered over to the door opposite. Before she reached the door, her head spun uncontrollably and she passed out.

Iz awakened to find Spencer dragging her through the door into the next room. The walls and ceiling of the room were covered in human faeces. The smell was nauseating. Iz almost passed out again as the stench assaulted her senses. Spencer pulled Iz into the centre of the room and stopped. The room suddenly felt freezing, and she thought back to that winter night when she dropped Adam. He was a few months old, and she didn't want to hold onto him. She had no feelings for babies. Her mother insisted that Iz took Adam from her. When her mother turned around to buy hot doughnuts, Iz opened her arms and let Adam fall to the ground. Everyone would have thought it was an accident if it hadn't been for the man sitting on the park bench watching her. He told the police that Iz had deliberately dropped Adam. She never realised it at the time, but now she knew it was Spencer who told them.

Spencer got down on all fours and crawled over to a corner of the room.

"I'm sorry," he said.

He sat facing the corner and rocked back and forth, humming a lullaby that Iz remembered her mother used to sing to Adam to calm him.

"Do you know how many little stars..."

Adam had always been a fretful baby. He always cried. Iz was sure he only cried to annoy her.

Spencer stopped singing. "Do you know how the senses can be tormented?" he said. "What you smell, see, hear, or taste can be worse than what you physically feel. It is your mind that holds the greatest fears. Everything begins and ends in the mind, except the soul. The soul is different. Clever. Immune. It hides someplace other than in the mind."

"What place?" Iz asked, covering her nose and mouth with her hand.

"The liver."

Standing, Iz stared down at Spencer. He was singing the lullaby again and rocking back and forth. The stench in the room was unbearable. She made her way towards the door and opened it.

Spencer sat naked in the centre of the next room. Both his ears had been cut off. His mouth was stitched shut with coarse thread. Blood dripped down his neck.

"You can call me Snake," he said.

His lips did not move but Iz heard his voice clearly, like it was talking inside her head.

She stepped into the room and the door closed behind her. The man said his name was Snake, but she knew it was Spencer.

"Will you kiss me, Izabella?" he said.

"Tell me what this is all about?" Iz said. "Are you a clone?"

"You have never felt like you fit in anywhere, have you? And you have always felt special."

"No," Iz said.

"Do not worry. You do not have a mental disorder, despite what they said about you in the asylum. You were not shaped by your environment like the sociopath. Your character is set deep within your blood, your soul. It is as natural as the colour of your eyes."

Iz looked around the room as Spencer continued talking. The walls and ceiling were covered with newspaper articles. All the stories related to some form of atrocity. Gun massacres, torture houses, and genocide filled the black and white pages. The floor was also covered in newspaper pages. She stared at the man. "Who cut off your ears?" she asked.

"Psychopaths are yesterday's news, yesterday's nightmares. Soon there will be more psychopaths roaming the streets than normal people."

Iz checked the corners of the room, looking for the man's ears.

"In today's society," he continued, *"everyone has mental health issues. Everyone is desensitised to atrocity. How boring."*

"Where are your ears?" Iz asked.

"The world needs a new breed of monster, a new kind of psychopath. The world needs someone like you, Izabella. Someone who can show the true potential of the sharded."

"Sharded like me."

Iz walked over to the man and checked his pockets. His ears were in his left pocket. She pulled them out and stared at them, then put them in her own pocket.

"Are you going to sew them back on?" the man asked.

"I don't have a needle and thread."

The man strained against the thread and managed to pull his lips apart. Iz stared into his mouth and saw a sewing pin pierced his tongue.

Iz bent down in front of Spencer and picked the remaining thread from his lips. When it was all removed, she put the thread in her pocket. Then she opened Spencer's mouth, pulled the sewing pin from his tongue, and pinned it to her coat collar.

A cracking sound, like a tree branch had been broken in half.

Spencer's head fell backwards and his lower jaw came apart from his upper jaw. Sharded blood, like fragments of broken glass, burst out of his mouth. The bloody shards hit Iz directly in her face and, like fingers, the shards wrapped themselves around her head. They slowly drew her face into Spencer's broken jaws. Iz attempted to pull herself away from Spencer but could not. The taste of blood, too strong. The sound of dogs barking, too loud. The smell of excrement, too acrid. The view of darkness, too black. The touch of fingers against her skull. Crushing. Penetrating. Devouring her every secret.

"Will you be my girlfriend? I want you to give me children."

The blood became liquified and fell to the floor. Iz pulled herself away from Spencer and stood up. Spencer sat in front of her. His mouth gaped open as tendrils of blood squirmed out of it, desperately searching for something Iz could not imagine.

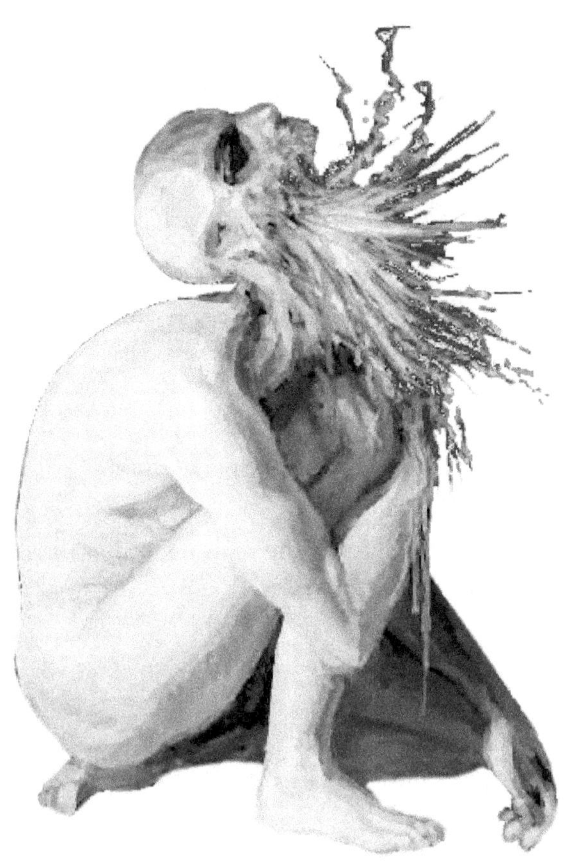

Iz walked over to the door and saw it opened into a basilica. A priest knelt at an altar, praying. Iz entered and the door closed. She couldn't make out what the priest was saying, but from his body shape and hair, she knew it was Spencer.

Behind the altar, was the font where she was supposed to take the picture.

"Spencer," she said.

He turned to face her, continuing to pray as he did. His ears were not missing. His lips were not stitched together.

"Could you take a photo of me while I take a piss in the font?" Iz said.

Spencer smiled. He stood up and walked over to Iz. She handed him the phone. He took it from her and backed away, positioning himself so that he could take the photograph.

Iz walked over to the font and pulled her jeans and panties down. She hoisted herself onto the font and sat over it. A moment later, the only sound was urine hitting the holy water in the font.

Spencer took a single photograph.

When she was finished, Iz dropped down from the font and put her panties and jeans back on. She took the phone from him and studied the picture he had taken.

"The world needs more like you," Spencer said.

"What's so special about me?"

"You have the potential to be the nightmare that man has always needed to guide him towards God."

"How do I get out of here?"

"Through the door," Spencer said, pointing towards the rear of the basilica behind the altar.

Iz made a move towards the door but stopped and turned towards the man. "Why all these rooms?" she asked. "What have you been trying to show me?"

"Not show *you*, show *me*. I needed to confirm you were the person I hoped you were."

She took some gum out of her pocket and put it in her mouth.

"I have something better you can chew on," Spencer said.

"I don't do sex acts for perverts."

"A wasted opportunity, for sure, but that's not what I meant. I was offering you one of my ears."

"Your words bore me."

Spencer laughed. "Stitch up my mouth and your destiny will pass you by."

Iz took the sewing needle and thread from her pocket. Standing in front of Spencer, she pierced his lower lip with the needle. He flinched and continued to flinch each time the needle pierced his skin but made no attempt to stop her.

"I don't know why that gave me so much pleasure," she said, when she finished stitching his lips together.

After studying her handy work, she walked over to the door and twisted the knob. The door was locked. She turned towards Spencer. "I want to leave," she said.

"And I want you to eat these," he said, without his lips moving.

Iz heard the voice inside her head.

Pulling a pair of scissors from his robe, Spencer proceeded to cut off each of his ears. Blood streamed down the sides of his face as he offered the ears to Iz.

"Why would I want to eat those?" Iz asked.

"Because they will make you beautifully immortal."

"I don't want to live forever."

"You will after you eat my ears."

Iz felt inside her pockets. She could not find the ears she took from the Spencer in the previous room. She walked up to the priest; certain he would not allow her to leave until she performed his tricks. "I'll eat one if you eat one," she said.

Iz took the bloodied scissors from him and cut the thread tying his lips together.

Spencer grinned. "My god, you are perfect."

He offered one of his ears to Iz and she took it from him. She looked at the ear, turned it around in her hand, then placed it in her mouth and began chewing.

Spencer did the same with the other ear.

"What now?" Iz asked after she swallowed.

He chewed a little longer on his ear, then swallowed it.

"You have always had a desire to eat human flesh, Izabella. Since you first became aware when just a baby, sucking on your mother's breast. That is when I first became aware of you. The only thing you got wrong was which part of a human you needed to eat to get the most satisfaction. The heart and the brain may seem like obvious choices, in fact, it is the liver that provides the only sustenance you will ever require. It is not only the largest gland in the human body, but also the seat of the human soul. That is what makes it so special. That is what makes it your prime goal. Do you understand?"

Iz felt nauseous, dizzy. Bored with his monotonous talk. She dropped to her knees, unable to stand. Lights flashed inside her head. Still, she heard his voice drone.

"I have found another just like you, dearest Izabella. Unlike you, he has spent his life fighting his true nature. Not anymore."

Waves of blackness pulsed through Iz.

The waves washed everything away. Images of her life flashed before her and settled on the jock who broke his leg during a match. She had always been fascinated with human bones. His thigh bone jutted out from his leg like a sharded spear, and his leg was twisted at an impossible angle. The impossibility excited Iz and she couldn't believe how white the bone looked. She loved the contrast of white bone against red blood. She wanted to lick the thigh bone clean while carving the remaining flesh off the rest of the leg. Carve the flesh off the foot too, and each individual toe. She could suck the toes clean afterwards. It would be cool to use an electric carving knife. Thinking about it, she could almost feel the blade vibrating in her hand and hear the motor buzz in her ears as she made her choice.

More light flashed across her eyes.

A groaning and a creaking filled her ears as her skull contorted and morphed into a new shape. All her hair dropped out as her mouth widened and her jaw snapped, leaving a gaping hole that looked nothing like a mouth. She raised her hands to her face and stared as her fingers doubled in length right in front of her eyes.

"I want you to meet him, Izabella. Meet him and bear his child. But first, you have another job to complete. You need to make everyone who has a soul like yours the same as I have made you today. Do you understand, Izabella? Feed them your flesh like I fed you mine. Let the sharded make themselves known to all."

The mutation ceased and Iz panted like a dog on her hands and knees. Everything had changed. Everything she could see around her, each sound, the touch of the ground beneath her hands, tastes within her mouth, were all amplified. But it was the scent inside her broken nose that affected her most. The scent of something coming from the man. Still on her hands and knees, she crawled over to him. At his feet, she sniffed, up his leg, his abdomen, just below his right ribcage, where the scent was strongest.

"It's overwhelming, isn't it, Mummy?" the man said.

Iz stood up and stared at her hands. Her fingers were like sharded claws rather than fingers. Their tips as sharp as black thorns. The scent hit her senses again and she could not stop herself from using her claws to rip open the man's robes and the flesh beneath. She tore at his flesh until she found that sweet gland below and pulled it from his abdomen.

Spencer fell to the ground, but he did not scream. He stared at Iz for as long as he could until his eyes closed and all life left the body he had possessed.

Iz no longer noticed the man. The only thing on her mind was the glistening organ she held in her hands. Its scent was now a visible mist that rose and wound a spiralling path towards her. She bit into the liver and blood spurted from it, spraying her hands and body, while more dripped from her mouth. The warmth of the liver, combined with its taste, forced her to close her eyes and lose herself in everything that was liver.

The warmth. The taste. The smell.

She bit and bit again, until there was no more liver in her hands and her belly was full of the mana essence of liver. She opened her eyes and saw the man on the floor, dead. The scent again. It came from outside. Not the same as the liver she had just devoured. This scent was more pungent, more alluring. It came from a dozen human livers sitting around a campfire. She knew what she had to do.

A noise behind. She turned around. A door had opened. It led to the outside world.

Something else.

Another, the same as her. The same, but far away, across an ocean. It didn't matter. She would figure it out and find him later. For now, there was the scent of liver and the urge to make more people sharded. People whose liver reeked of the same dark soul essence that her own liver possessed.

Zaire

The kid wouldn't look anyone in the eyes. He stared at the ground, spitting. Over and over, he spat at the ground. No gob came out of his mouth. He could have been spitting all day long for all Zaire knew. Maybe his mouth had dried up or something. The youths surrounding him laughed. It made no difference to the kid. He couldn't seem to tell the difference between a smiling face and an angry face.

One of the youths poked the kid with a stick. He poked him in the leg, the arm, the ribs. He slapped him across the face, hard. The slap reverberated around the alley. No one made a sound as the youths looked anxiously at each other.

The kid rocked back and forth on his heels as a red welt extended across his cheek.

Zaire stared, fascinated by the kid.

"Let's put something in his mouth to stop him spitting," Stick Youth said.

"What?" A red-haired kid in the group asked.

"Does anyone want to take a shit?"

The group laughed nervously.

"I do," the smallest one of them said.

Stick Youth smiled. "Go on then, but don't do it in front of us. Go behind those trash cans over there and bring your shit back in a plastic bag. You can get one out of the trash."

Zaire had only ever seen someone eat shit once before. She did it for drugs; her dealer wanted to prove a point to his employees. He didn't want to see anyone eat shit again. He finished his smoke, stubbed it out on the ground with his foot, and walked towards the alley exit.

Stick Youth pushed the kid. He pushed him until the kid fell to the ground on his knees. He started to whip the kid's ass with the stick.

A pile of rubble had been dumped near where the kid knelt. He crawled over to it and pulled broken bricks out of the rubble. He began to stack the bricks on top of each other.

Zaire's stomach churned.

He stopped walking.

The youth came back from the trash cans a moment later. He held his shit out in front of himself wrapped in an old newspaper. His free hand covered his nose, and he gurned his face as he approached them.

The others saw him and laughed.

Zaire continued to watch the kid stack the bricks. He was slow and meticulous as he placed one brick on top of another. Something happened inside Zaire's head as he watched. He walked over to the kid and knelt beside him, taking a closer look at his face.

"Put it on the floor," Stick Youth said to the one carrying the shit.

The gang huddled around the turd as it was carefully placed on the ground. It was bent like a large banana, and black like a Djarum cigar. They stared at it for a moment as if it was sacred. Stick Youth pressed the end of the stick into the turd and raised it up in front of himself, studying it closely.

The gang stepped back from him.

"What the hell?" Stick Youth said to the one whose turd he held at the end of the stick. "This shit is big enough to have come out of a full-grown man's asshole."

Laughter.

The group followed as Stick Youth walked over to the kid stacking bricks.

Zaire turned around and stood to his full height as Stick Youth approached.

"Fuck off out of here," Zaire told him.

Stick Youth hesitated a moment. "He needs to eat shit," he finally said.

"Why?" Zaire asked.

"Can't you see he's a disgusting fuck?"

"I can see *you* are a nasty little fuck," Zaire said. "I want to see you eat the shit."

The other youths backed away from Stick Youth. He looked around nervously. "That's not gonna happen," he said to Zaire, without any conviction.

Zaire lunged at Stick Youth and slapped him hard across his face. Tears formed in his eyes as the force of the blow knocked him backwards.

"You just made the biggest mistake of your life," Stick Youth weakly said. "Don't you know who I am?"

"Bro," one of the gang members said to Stick Youth, "that's Zaire Rooney."

Stick Youth tensed, placed the stick on the ground, and backed away from Zaire. The others followed and made their way to the end of the alley. They stopped before they exited the alley and began to beat Stick Youth.

"What are you called anyway?" Zaire said to the kid stacking bricks.

"Doctor Who," the kid said.

"You think you are Doctor Who?"

"Doctor Who," the kid repeated.

"I don't like the Doctor. I'll call you Dalek or Cyber, after the Cyber Men. What do you think?"

"Doctor Who," the kid said.

"Fine, Dalek it is."

Zaire turned around, heading out of the alley. At the exit, he turned around again and stared at Dalek, who searched the rubble for more bricks to stack. Zaire made his way back to the kid. When he reached him, he grabbed hold of his arm, attempting to pull him up from the dirt.

The kid pulled away from him. "No. No. No," he shouted.

Zaire pulled harder on his arm and the kid shouted louder. He released his grip on him and the kid started to rummage around in the rubble, searching for bricks that were not there. Zaire saw a cloth sack partially buried in the rubble. He picked it up and shook it as clean as he could. He put the cloth over Dalek's head. The kid sat perfectly still when his head was covered with the sack. Zaire grabbed hold of his hand and pulled him up from the rubble, heading back towards the alleyway exit.

He walked him to the squat.

At the squat, Zaire took the sack off Dalek's head and the kid began to rock back and forth. The squat was an abandoned cathedral in the centre of the city. It was vast inside. The omnipresent silence was Zaire's favourite part of the structure. That and the washed-out Correggio inspired fresco on the dome above, depicting God in Heaven with his angels. Zaire had cleared out the other vagrants a few weeks previously and now stayed there alone. Staring at the kid, he briefly considered selling him to the meat grinders.

"Stop doing that, Dalek," Zaire said.

Dalek continued to rock and a moment later, he spat on the floor. He didn't stop spitting, even after his mouth had dried out again.

Zaire remembered how he had stacked bricks in the alleyway.

Making his way to a large, stone sarcophagus at the far wall, Zaire struggled to push the tomb lid to one side, but eventually managed to shift it far enough so he could reach inside and pull out a rucksack. He walked over to Dalek and took two cans of peaches from the rucksack. He placed the cans at his feet. Dalek stopped spitting. He stopped rocking. A moment later, he sat down and stacked one of the cans on top of the other. Zaire gave him another can from the rucksack and the kid stacked that on top of the two other cans. He looked up at Zaire, avoiding his eyes. Zaire emptied the sack and handed the remaining cans over to Dalek. Once he had stacked all the cans, he held out his hand for more.

"I'm all out of cans," Zaire said.

The kid began to grind his teeth.

Zaire picked the sack up from the floor and put it on the kid's head.

The grinding stopped.

Zaire removed the sack from Dalek's head the next day when he awakened and saw that the kid had pissed himself. Zaire slapped the kid across the face and told him not to piss himself ever again. Dalek began to cry and rocked backwards and forwards. Zaire gave him the cans of peaches. Dalek stacked the cans and when he finished, Zaire kicked the can tower over. The kid built the tower up again and again, after Zaire kept knocking it over. In the end, Dalek pushed the tower over himself and immediately started the building process once more.

"What do you eat?" Zaire said sometime later.

"Doctor Who," Dalek said.

Zaire took one of the cans of peaches off Dalek and opened it with his knife. Dalek watched anxiously as Zaire handed the peaches over to him. He quickly ate the peaches and stacked the empty can on top of the tower. He stared at the tower for a moment, and then knocked it over with a swipe of his hand.

He began to build the tower again.

"Where do you live?" Zaire said after he had eaten a can of corned beef and smoked a roll-up.

"Tardis," the kid said.

"Shit," Zaire said.

Laying on a grimy mattress, Zaire closed his eyes and slept. When he awakened a few hours later, he lit the space with two 8-inch candles. He stared at Dalek who continued to stack cans. He had always liked the silence inside the cathedral at night-time and the smell of burning candle wax. Listening to the sound of the cans as they clinked together, Zaire found a new favourite sound.

A scream.

Zaire opened his eyes and saw the kid in front of the drawing. He quickly got up and dashed over to Dalek. He turned him away from the drawing and the kid calmed down a little.

"You don't like the sharded? Don't fret, no one likes them."

He walked the kid over to the cans and sat him down. Dalek stacked the cans.

Zaire went back to the drawing. It was one of Aasim's best. He rolled it up and put it under the mattress. It reminded Zaire of a laughing dog rather than a sharded. If only he could go back to the days when Aasim drew angels instead of sharded.

"I need to go make money," Zaire said.

The kid continued to stack cans.

"It can wait until tomorrow," he said, as he lit a roll up, lay on the mattress, and stared at the fresco above as it moved in the shifting candlelight.

"You can't stay with me," Zaire said to Dalek the next day.

The kid had just finished eating a can of peaches.

"You need to toughen up so you can look after yourself."

Dalek stood by the sarcophagus, rocking back and forth. He spat on the floor. Zaire had taken the cans off him earlier and put them inside the sarcophagus.

"Clench your fists and put them in front of your face," Zaire said.

Dalek continued to rock and spit.

Zaire punched him in the face.

"Defend yourself," he said.

Dalek placed a hand on his cheek where he had been hit and started to cry.

Zaire hit him again, in the stomach this time. "Those other kids will do worse than this," he said.

Dalek stopped crying and spat on the floor.

Zaire breathed deeply. He took a knife out of the sheath strapped to his ankle. "Here," he said, "take this."

The kid spat on the floor.

Zaire put the knife in the kid's hand.

The kid dropped the knife on the floor and spat on it.

Zaire picked up the knife, wiped it clean on his trousers, and put it back in the sheath. He got the sack from the floor and put it over Dalek's head.

He lit a roll up.

He didn't know what to do with the kid.

The next morning, Zaire took Dalek back to the alleyway. It was deserted. He removed the sack from Dalek's head. The kid looked around and saw the bricks. He walked over to them, sat down, and began to stack them.

"Someone must be looking for you. Maybe they will come here. Remember what I said about those other kids. Hit them twice as hard as they hit you and you won't have any more trouble with them."

Zaire left Dalek to go and make money, thinking that the sound of bricks being stacked wasn't as relaxing as the sound of cans being stacked. Hustling the girls on Princess Street, he couldn't get the kid out of his thoughts. Later, once he had traded cash for cans of corned beef and peaches, he didn't want to return to the squat by the alley route. It was raining. If he took a detour away from the alley, he would be drenched by the time he got back to the squat. He was drenched anyway.

It was dark. He didn't see Dalek until he was almost on top of him. He heard the brick tower collapse before he saw the kid. Even in the dim light, Zaire saw that his clothes were drenched and his hair was plastered to his scalp. Strands of it hung down his forehead, partially covering his eyes.

"No one came for you, huh?" Zaire said.

Dalek stopped what he was doing and looked up at him. He grabbed hold of Zaire's legs and hugged them.

He pulled Dalek off his legs.

The kid started to wail and went back to stacking bricks.

"Shit."

Zaire tried to grab his hand, but the kid brushed him aside. He only wanted to stack bricks.

"Can't you see when someone is trying to help you?"

The kid did not respond.

"Fine," Zaire said, making his way to the exit.

At the end of the alleyway, he turned around and headed back towards the kid. He searched the ground when he reached him, looking for the sack. When he found it, he put the sack on the kid's head and took him back to the squat.

He tried to feed Dalek peaches, but he wouldn't eat. The kid shook uncontrollably and wouldn't open his eyes. He should never have been left alone in the rain. Zaire covered the kid in tarpaulin and lit a fire with wood from what remained of the cathedral seating. The crackle and pop of burning wood was almost as relaxing as cans being stacked. He force-fed peaches to the kid for two days even though he expected him to die in the cold of the night. The kid's fever broke on the third day. He was stacking cans again on the fourth day and Zaire was addicted to the sounds the kid made by the end of the fifth day.

"We need to make money, Dalek," Zaire said.

Zaire was famished. He didn't have any tokens to buy more corned beef or peaches. He listened to Dalek stacking cans one last time before taking him outside into the street. The kid was getting used to him, so there was no need to us the sack. He put it in his pocket anyway and made his way to the embankment. He hadn't been there for weeks. It was safer that way, keeping one step ahead of the pimps by varying his movements across the city. Three girls stood by the river. Zaire waited until they were alone, no punters or pimps around. He approached the prostitutes.

One of them recognised him.

"You're a dead man," she said. "When Ngezi finds you, he'll split you open with a knife and pull your guts out with his bare hands."

"Give me the tokens," Zaire said as he pulled the knife from the sheath. "Or it will be you who is split open."

The girls did not put up a fight. They never did; not after he slashed the face of the last one who refused to hand over her tokens. They knew Zaire by reputation. Reputation counted for more than reality.

"Take all my tokens," a girl with purple hair said. "I don't need them anyway."

"What do you mean?" Zaire asked.

"The sharded broke through the city defences last night. Soon we will all be like them, or dead."

"The sharded can't get past barbed wire and guns."

"Guns are useless without bullets," the girl said. "Every soldier who came to visit these past few weeks said they have more tokens than bullets. They act like frightened children in the playground. They have seen with their own eyes what the sharded do to anyone not strong enough to fight back. Trust me, they will use their last bullet on themselves, not the sharded."

If her words were true, Zaire knew he would have to leave the city. He looked down at Dalek. He didn't like the way the kid stared back at him. He put the sack over the kid's head and left the girls.

At the meat grinder, he took the sack off the kid's head and stared into his eyes.

The kid stared at the floor.

"We need to eat," Zaire said. "Without tokens, we cannot eat. That's why I have to take them from working girls. There is no other way for people like you and me to earn tokens."

Dalek spat on the floor.

Zaire pulled him through the doorway leading into the meat grinders. Before things changed, it had been a slaughterhouse. It was still a slaughterhouse, but now it was also a place of trade. Zaire led the kid to the wooden counter at the back of the gloomy space. The usual man who served wasn't there. A tall, thin man wearing a blood-stained apron stood in his place. Zaire guessed he was one of the butchers who filled the cans.

"Where is the old man?" Zaire asked when he reached the counter.

"Times are hard," the man said, leaning into the counter and facing them. "He traded himself in so his daughter could eat." The man looked Dalek up and down. "He will fetch fifty tokens. No more."

"He's not for sale," Zaire said.

"Not today, at least," the butcher said.

Zaire looked down at the kid, then back at the butcher. "I have tokens and I need peaches and corned beef."

"There are no more peaches," the man said.

"No more?"

"That's right, nothing grows in the city anymore, not even peaches. There is only corned beef for sale now."

Everyone called it corned beef. Everyone knew there was no beef inside the tin. There was only one kind of meat available in the city these days.

Zaire laid all the tokens on the counter.

The man started to place cans of corned beef on the counter. He stopped placing them on the counter when there were nine cans present.

"There are eighteen tokens," Zaire said. "There should be eighteen cans."

"Times are hard," the man said. "Take it or leave it."

Dalek stood on his tiptoes and started to stack the cans on the counter.

Zaire waited until Dalek had stacked all the cans, then he put the sack on the kid's head. He placed the cans in the rucksack and left the grinder's, heading for the squat.

The kid's eyes were closed and he sat, rocking back and forth. Zaire thought he must be famished. Despite all his attempts to get the kid to eat, Dalek would not eat corned beef. He stood up and walked over to the sarcophagus, reached inside, and pulled out the viddy. He pressed the button, but it was out of power again. He walked over to the patch of sunlight that entered through the hole in the dome. He placed the viddy on the floor and waited for the sunshine to recharge it.

When it was fully charged, Zaire picked it up and sat down opposite the kid. His mother had password protected it. He didn't know the password. He typed his name into the viddy. He knew it wasn't the correct password. He typed Aasim's name into it. He knew that was not the password either.

He put the viddy down and slept.

When Zaire awakened, he heard Doctor Who. He looked across at Dalek and saw that he had the viddy on his lap, staring at the screen.

Dalek had cracked the password.

Zaire got up and sat down beside Dalek. He was unsurprised to see the kid was watching Blink. It was the only Doctor Who episode on the viddy.

"How did you know the password?" Zaire said.

Dalek didn't respond.

Zaire stared at the weeping angels on the screen and images from his past swamped his mind. When the episode finished, he went to take the viddy off Dalek, but the kid held onto it tightly. With it still on Dalek's lap, Zaire flicked through the library. He stopped at Aasim.

He pressed play.

He stared at his older brother as he lay on the floor of their apartment stacking toy building blocks. He stared at the screen for five more minutes until the video ended. He realised then that he couldn't remember what his mother looked like. He remembered the day she took Aasim to the meat grinders. She couldn't make enough tokens on the embankment to feed two kids. Not when she had a habit to feed as well.

"Aasim can't look after himself like you can," his mother said that day. "It's him or you."

Zaire did not want to go to the meat grinders.

It was true, his brother could not look after himself. He was great at drawing, and he never lied. It was like he was wired that way, not able to lie even if his wellbeing depended on it. He could not look after himself even though he could draw the most amazing pictures of God in Heaven with his angels. No one was interested in drawings these days. No one had a use for Aasim.

Zaire remembered taking his mother to the meat grinders not long after she had sold Aasim to them. She was so out of it she didn't know where she was anyway. He never said goodbye to his mother.

He never said goodbye to Aasim.

Zaire switched the viddy off and Dalek started to grind his teeth. He switched it back on and watched Dalek enter the password. It was not what he expected. He would never have guessed the password. He knew Dalek didn't guess it either. He knew Dalek had figured out the password. Dalek was good at puzzles like Aasim was good at drawing.

It was night-time when Zaire heard them enter the cathedral. He got up and placed the sack cloth on Dalek's head. Despite the kid being sleepy and weak through starvation, he managed to walk him over to the rubble in the chancel where he covered him with the tarpaulin.

"Goodbye, Doctor Who," he said to the kid.

By the time he had made his way to the sarcophagus, he saw the men. There were three of them. One of the men shone a torch at Zaire.

"Over here," the man with the torch yelled.

Ngezi.

"You won't get away this time," Ngezi said. "Tonight, it's gonna be broken bones. Payback time."

Zaire ran towards the hole in the wall at the rear of the cathedral and scrambled though it into the night. Ngezi and his two bodyguards followed close behind. Zaire ran as fast as he could through the derelict city streets. He could hear the men behind him. They didn't talk or shout out loud, he simply heard their footsteps in the rubble. Zaire did not want to eat alone, so he hadn't eaten for two days. He was physically exhausted. They caught up with him two blocks from the cathedral and pushed him to the ground.

"You really thought it was a good idea to steal from me, boy?" Ngezi said, kicking Zaire in the stomach. "You're fucking with my reputation. Everyone thinks I'm a soft touch because of you. Not after tonight. Not after I cut off your arms and legs and string your body from that butt ugly cathedral."

Blows came in from all directions. Zaire knew he wouldn't survive the night. He knew he was dead the first time he stole from Ngezi. He thought about Dalek. He liked the fact the kid would not eat corned beef. Aasim would never eat corned beef either. His mother had to force feed him meat. There was something special about Dalek and Aasim. They were not the same as everyone else. They didn't belong in the city. Zaire wasn't sure where they belonged. He knew Dalek would never move from underneath the tarpaulin as long as the sack remained on his head. At least he would not end up where Zaire was heading. The grinders would never crush the kid's bones to a pulp. He wished he could say the same about Aasim.

Screams.

Not screams, wailings, from the darkness. Inhuman, but human all the same. It was true; the sharded were in the city.

The men stopped beating him, yet the pain pulsing through his body intensified.

His attackers ran. They were not fast enough. Their screams joined the wailing of the sharded.

They soon stopped.

The sound of flesh being torn apart. Squelching next as the sharded ate the men's livers. No one knew why the sharded only ate the liver. Everyone expected a zombie attack to end with the brains being eaten. The sharded were not zombies.

Silence.

Rustling nearby.

Footsteps.

Something approached. It kneeled beside Zaire. Staring up, he saw its sharded head silhouetted against the night sky. Its shoulders were sharded too, and part of its left arm. That was odd, in all the pictures he had seen of the sharded, their heads were the only part of their bodies that were deformed.

"They didn't seem to like you, friend," it said.

"You can talk," Zaire said.

"I can take a shit as well, what's your point?"

Zaire wanted to ask if its shit was sharded too but thought that was a bad idea.

It bent down and sniffed Zaire's ear, his nose, his mouth. It licked his eyes. "Want to join us?" it finally said.

Zaire felt dazed from the beating, maybe he heard wrong. "What?"

More movement in the darkness. Another sharded appeared. Two more, three. Soon, all Zaire could see were sharded all around.

"I asked if you wanted to join us. Do you want to become like us?"

Zaire didn't want to become sharded. They would take his liver if he refused, though. He thought about Dalek. He didn't want him to die of starvation, alone in the cathedral, stacking bricks in his head until the end.

"What do I have to do?"

The sharded chewed on its left arm.

Zaire sat up and winced at the pain.

"Eat this," the sharded said, offering him the flesh it had chewed off its arm.

Zaire took the flesh from it. "I have a friend," he said. "A young boy. He's a brother to me. Can he join us too?"

"It depends how he smells," the sharded said.

Zaire put the flesh in his mouth. He chewed. It tasted like corned beef. He swallowed.

"Will he stay a child if he is turned?"

"No, he will grow up to be big and strong, just like you."

The pain slowly diminished until there was no pain at all. Then, the real pain came. Zaire screamed like never before. His vision blurred and was quickly replaced by intense light blazing across his eyes. His skull stretched and twisted, making terrible creaking sounds. Raising his hands to his head, he felt the shards growing ever larger from the left side of his face and the top of his skull. Now his shoulders and arms pulsed in transformation as they convulsed and sharded until he had not one left arm, but four. He felt swelling in his neck and placed his hand there. He felt a gaping mouth with sharp teeth protruding from it at awkward angles. The transformation stopped as quickly as it began.

There was no more pain, only heightened senses. A strong scent came from the sharded one whose flesh he had eaten. The scent came from the other sharded ones who surrounded him. Zaire too, smelled the same. He could hear thoughts within his mind, thoughts that were not his own. He stood up and looked around. The darkness held no secrets from him. The shadows illuminated everything like torch-light in the night. Images of his past life flashed through his mind. The first, his mother smiling into his face one sunny day on the beach. The last, a boy stacking cans inside a ruined cathedral. The images quickly waned, as if they would never return. They were replaced with something more important. A sense that some being watched over him. A presence that felt as real to Zaire as his newly formed shards.

The Sweet Scent of Liver

"Who is it that watches over us?" he asked.

No one answered.

They waited a moment longer and then, as one, strode towards the agonisingly sweet scent coming from the city. Zaire followed them for a short while, then stopped beside a huge structure with large, arched windows. The scent was all around, pungent and alluring. Up ahead, the smell was strongest and most plentiful. That was why the others headed in that direction. Something other than the scent made Zaire enter the structure. A memory? He wasn't sure. His eyes scanned the area towards a covering on the ground. He walked towards it and lifted the covering. The vaguely familiar shape of a small human lay on the ground with a sack over its head.

The human's scent filled him with deep yearning.

He took the sack off its head. A young boy looked up, his eyes stared wildly at him.

Then he hugged his legs.

"Doctor Who," he said.

Something... something... something.

Nothing.

He took the boy's head in his hands and twisted. His neck snapped easily and he slumped to the ground.

Using his sharded teeth and five hands, he pulled away the skin just below the ribcage. The liver glistened back at him. He tore it from the body and held it in front of his face. The scent almost made him pass out. He sank his teeth into the organ.

"Now you are truly one of us," a voice inside his head spoke.

The watcher.

Zaire consumed the liver without answering. The liver essence spread though his body like the wildest bush fire. It felt like he was glowing as every particle within his being rejoiced.

And then, it was over, far too quickly.

"Go to Paris. Find the woman I guide you towards. Make her the same as you and me. Find others to help you. Do it soon. But not before the woman reaches the age of twenty-one. Do you understand?"

The scent, all around. Outside, Zaire's brothers and sisters fed. He needed to join them. Staring down at the boy, something washed through him. Sadness? It was gone as soon as it arrived. He picked up the sack and put it in his trouser pocket, then exited the building and followed the scent.

Ylang Ylang

York 2104

Ylang first saw the synthetic in Meticulous Meticulous on Sunday night when she served beer in champagne glasses to geneticists. The news about Zion had just broken and everyone thought it would be the end of the sharded. The synthetic was on her own, sitting at Ylang's favourite place in the corner beside the Peace Lily.

She did not like people sitting in her corner.

It may have been the synthetic's dark hair that drew Ylang to her. It was so straight and perfectly gleaming beneath the low wattage lighting. Just as easily, it could have been her melancholic eyes looking at nothing. Maybe it was neither of those things. Maybe it was the languid way she drank her vodka. How she brought the glass to her lips and swallowed perfunctorily like she wasn't taking any pleasure in the drink, merely demonstrating how easily she could force herself to do something she didn't enjoy.

Red light angled in through the window above the synthetic as the last tram squealed its arrival. The doors opened and two passengers stepped out of the carriage. Their heels echoed dully against the grey pavement. The synthetic suddenly looked toward the entrance. When no one entered, she didn't appear surprised.

"It was all a lie," the radio broadcaster announced. *"The sharded were not defeated. The third legion has been totally wiped out."*

People got up and started to leave. The synthetic did not get up. Instead, she ordered another drink. She had two more drinks before the bar closed.

Her artificial intelligence must have been on some trip, Ylang thought. She'd like to say that she didn't take advantage of the synthetic at closing time.

Her attraction was undeniable.

Taxis no longer ran after dark, not since the embargo. Ylang walked the synthetic the short distance to her apartment, located above a restoration store close to the derelict cathedral. It was expansive with double bay windows to the front, and four sets of sash windows to the rear. There were no rooms, no dividing walls. The lounge ran into the kitchen, the kitchen into the sleeping area, the sleeping area into the bathroom, the bathroom into the lounge. Glancing around the space, Ylang noticed a statue of David resting on the mantelpiece. It had been painted black. She could understand the need for someone to do that to him.

The synthetic walked over to the cube and pressed a button. Broken Bells streamed out from high-level speakers all around the apartment. It was like listening to music in 3D and Ylang could easily have spent the remainder of the night doing no more than losing herself in those three dimensions. The synthetic pulled Ylang into her space. She tasted of neat vodka and her synthetic skin held a suggestion of the bar. The scents of leather seat polish and constantly percolating coffee had found her and remained. She removed Ylang's clothes while remaining fully clothed herself. When she dragged her over to the bed, Ylang undressed the synthetic. She fell into unconsciousness just as Ylang removed her bra. Looking down at the synthetic's nakedness, Ylang briefly considered all the possibilities presented before her on the crisp white sheets. She stared at the synthetic's sleeping face, tried to see what it was that made her different from all the others, tried to understand her allure.

She could not name it.

Ylang walked over to the kitchen and opened the refrigerator door. A bowl of cherries gleamed like they had been buffed with leather chair polish. She grabbed the bowl and began eating the perfectly ripened fruit, spitting the stones back into the bowl. It was clear to see that the synthetic came from a powerful background. How else could she have fresh fruit in her fridge? At the cube, Ylang flicked through the playlist and saw, with some surprise, that she had similar tastes to the synthetic.

The wooden floor felt warm against the soles of her bare feet, like it was burning on the other side of the boards. Feeling a little queasy, she ran the cold tap in the granite sink and put her head underneath the flowing water. Cooler and clear of thought, she turned off the tap and dried her hair with the towel on the rail at the end of the counter.

After finishing the last of the cherries, she felt hot again. Perhaps she was coming down with a fever. Leaving the bowl of cherry stones on top of the circular dining table, she walked over to the bed and removed her panties. Lying on the bed next to the synthetic, Ylang moulded herself into the synthetic's back and naked slept the rest of the night away.

The next morning, Ylang watched the synthetic crawl across the bed towards her. The synthetic's expression was neither sultry nor interested. The early morning light came in through the gap between the blinds, shining through the strands of her hair as she crept closer, magnifying her beauty.

"I want you again," the synthetic said, mistakenly thinking they had sex the night before.

When she began to suck on her toe, Ylang did not think it right to tell her otherwise.

Afterward, they sat at the dining table eating croissants and strawberry jam.

"I don't even know your name," the synthetic said, blowing the steaming espresso she held in both hands while staring at Ylang eating her croissant.

"I'm called Ylang…"

"I think I'll call you Ylang Ylang."

"What should I call you?"

"Let's watch a movie," the synthetic said, rising from her seat and heading into the lounge area with her espresso left untouched on the table.

Ylang Ylang sat on the walnut canapé sofa while she flicked through the synthetic's movie collection. The sofa looked elegant, but it was impossible to get comfortable on the wicker seating and ornate frame. Holographic technology was no longer freely available. Film reel was the fashionable alternative. The projector whirred into life, and Ylang Ylang watched it light up the large screen while the synthetic walked over to the bay windows and closed the blinds. In the darkness, the synthetic wordlessly sat next to Ylang Ylang and then pressed buttons on the controller. After a short while, *Institute Benjamenta* appeared on the screen in glorious black and white. Ylang Ylang was immediately drawn into the movie's sounds. The creak of leather as the servants swayed their way toward Alice affected her profoundly. It got inside her skull and eroticised. The way Alice talked when she asked her young saplings to refer to their manual—like a synthetic breathing into her ear while she slept—tingled her scalp. When they watched Alice cut herself with the deer hoof, Ylang Ylang's newfound lover squeezed her hand so tight that she wanted to kiss her painfully.

"Did you like Alice?" Ylang Ylang asked when the movie finished.

"Yes." The synthetic smiled. Sad, still, but pleased.

"Can I call you Alice?" Ylang asked.

"Yes. Yes, I'd like that."

Alice rested her head on Ylang Ylang's shoulder then and closed her eyes. "I want to dream in black and white," she said.

"What do you want to dream about?"

"I want to be a sapling."

"A servant?"

"I don't want to have to make any more decisions."

"Decisions about what?

Alice didn't reply.

Ylang Ylang was certain Alice pretended to sleep. She closed her eyes too. Unsure where Alice was taking her, she did not care. How Alice made her feel was everything. Cocooned inside her apartment, she never wanted to leave.

Ylang Ylang awakened sometime later with Alice still regenerating against her shoulder, giving her pins and needles. It didn't matter, she didn't want to be anywhere else. She should have been back at the bar, but Meticulous Meticulous was just a job. Alice was something she had never experienced before.

Alice stirred, raising her head from Ylang Ylang's shoulder.

"The sharded are so beautiful," Alice said dreamily. Her head shifted, then. Twisted, grew larger. Her jaw extended and her eyes became slanted pools of black loveliness. Her hair morphed into creamy white shards that formed a skull-like beehive. She opened her mouth and a large tongue flicked out of it and licked her now sharded teeth.

Ylang Ylang was shocked. She had heard about shape shifting synthetics, but never encountered one before. It both frightened her and prickled her spine with electric pleasure.

"You are beautiful," she said.

Alice smiled. "Do you like Turkish food?" she said.

"Yes."

She got up and stretched, went to the restored pay phone hanging next to the front door, and ordered takeaway.

"We have an hour before it arrives," Alice said. "Time enough to bathe."

Alice sat behind Ylang Ylang in the bath with her wet, glistening legs on either side of her chest. She washed Ylang Ylang's hair with shampoo and the fragrance reminded her of a girl she liked in college. When Alice rinsed her hair with the shower head, her synthetic fingers were as light as the wind and almost caressed Ylang Ylang back to sleep. Later, Alice dried her with a white cotton towel as she stood in front of her. Alice dressed her in one of her own bath gowns, while Ylang Ylang concentrated on the tips of her fingers, each time they inadvertently touched her skin.

"Why are you no longer sharded?" Ylang Ylang asked.

"Beauty loses its appeal if it comes out to play too often."

Sitting at the dining table, they drank pinot noir and listened to The Penguin Café Orchestra without speaking while waiting for the food. As expected, the meal arrived exactly one hour after Alice had ordered it. A teenage girl wearing a free issue Uprising T-shirt waited as Alice showed her ID. Ylang Ylang stared at the girl, trying to discern if there were any differences about the girl's face to her own. There were usually small variations. The girl wore a baseball cap instead of a motorcycle helmet, as part of her rebellious behaviour against the faction. Alice paid with correctly weighted coins. From her disposition, it was difficult to distinguish if the girl was synthetic or clone like Ylang Ylang.

Alice removed the food from the takeaway wrappings and served them on her perfectly white dishes. She sat opposite, drinking pinot noir, watching Ylang Ylang eat kashkek with cacik yoghurt and tandir bread.

"Why do you hate your studies?" she suddenly asked Ylang Ylang.

"Because I want to be a poet."

"You write poetry?"

"No. I don't know how to write poetry."

"Do you keep a journal?"

"No."

"I want you to write about your time here with me."

"Okay. Do you ever write?" Ylang Ylang asked Alice.

"Not anymore."

After she finished eating, Ylang Ylang made a move to wash the dishes.

"You are never to wash dishes," Alice said.

Ylang Ylang watched as Alice cleaned up the dishes from the table and put them in the sink. She rubbed them clean, and clean again, then simply continued to rub them with the cloth like she was doing something essentially profound. Watching her working this way filled Ylang Ylang with something she could only describe as adoration. She didn't want to stop Alice. It didn't feel like her place. She could see that Alice had slipped into temporal fugue, that was all, nothing serious. She eventually took the cloth away from Alice and guided her to bed. She needed rest, she needed Ylang Ylang. She closed her eyes without knowing she was doing so and slept as she reset.

Ylang Ylang picked up the journal Alice had given her and sat at the table, watching her breathe. She wished she could follow Alice into her dreams. She hated being apart from her. If only dream sequencing had not been prohibited after the sharded revelation. At least, prohibited for everyone except those in control. She closed her eyes and tried to imagine what Alice saw while she slept.

They were together, before the sharded and winter, before cloning spoiled everything. It was snowing and there was no sadness when it snowed here, no loss of innocence, only joyfulness. They heard bells, ringing out in the distance, but bells all the same. And there were men here too, like those they saw in movies, not the clones of today.

She opened her eyes.

The journal stared blankly back at her. Picking up the pen, she began to fill the journal with words about Alice. The scent of her skin, how she whispered in her sleep, the way her artificial eyes always betrayed her feelings. They had only been together a short while, yet Ylang Ylang understood her like nothing else she had ever encountered before. Never had writing come so easily to her, and reading the words she had written, it felt like at last she was writing poetry.

Poetry only she could understand.

At the refrigerator Ylang Ylang opened the door and picked up a jar of beetroot. Placing it on the dining room table, she moved toward the counter and the bread.

"Let me do that," Alice said behind her. "You are never to make food for yourself."

Alice had reset perfectly.

Ylang Ylang sat at the table and watched Alice prepare her sandwich.

"How is your writing going?"

"Fine, I really enjoy writing about us. Do you want me to read it to you?"

Alice placed the sandwich in front of her. "We need to go shopping. I want to buy you some clothes."

Biting into the sandwich, Ylang Ylang didn't taste anything, not even the synthetically produced olives inside. She didn't want to leave the apartment. Not even for a brief moment.

"Hurry, we need to set off before the sun falls," Alice said.

How could she want to go outside? Ylang Ylang didn't want to share her with anyone else. Something was wrong. She had miscalculated everything. "I think it is going to snow."

Alice walked to the window and placed her hand on the glass, staring outside. "It won't snow today."

When she took her hand away from the glass, Ylang Ylang watched her fingerprints disappear on the reflective surface. She didn't like seeing any part of Alice vanish. Her hands shook as she brought the sandwich to her mouth.

"I'm tired of seeing you in Meticulous Meticulous garb," Alice said. "Hurry up and finish eating."

Outside, the rain immediately began to touch Alice, making her wet. The wind thought Ylang Ylang couldn't see it caressing Alice, running its invisible fingers through her hair. She despised the wind and the rain, but it was the others who hurt the most, as she watched their eyes take Alice into those places she could not follow. The places she could only ever imagine.

Holding onto her hand, Alice led Ylang Ylang into the only store still selling clothes in the shopping precinct. Inside, Ylang Ylang gave the assistant, who looked exactly like her, a fierce gaze after she stared at Alice too long. Ylang Ylang wanted the assistant to look different to her, but as usual, the dissimilarities were miniscule, almost imperceptible. Cloning was too clever, like a mirror that never quite revealed everything, it kept secrets. You needed to stare at it from the mirror edge. Only then could you see how imprecise and cruel it had become.

A stuffed sharded man stood close to the entrance. It was bare chested with its wrists crossed and its hands clenched in defiant fists. Only its head and right arm were sharded. It had no discernible eyes and a mouth that comprised the whole of its face. The shop manager had dressed it in black combat trousers. She only ever dressed it in trousers, whatever the most fashionable trousers were each month. Rumour told that the sharded man was once a leader, one who took a human for a lover, a human who gave birth to a sharded child. The first, and only, time someone had been created in sharded form without eating sharded flesh. The child frightened the sharded and humans alike. That's why the man, his wife, and the child were slaughtered. No one knew where the mother's and child's bodies rested. Ylang Ylang stared at the creature. Something washed through her. Melancholy. For herself and the creature. She wished she could lay it to rest with its wife and child.

Alice scanned the clothing rails, taking various items from them before putting them back. Ylang Ylang agreed to the first clothes Alice chose for her. Alice paid for them with correctly weighted coins, and they walked out of the shop with Ylang Ylang dressed just the way Alice liked, in clothes far too elegant for a student wanting to hide.

"Can we go back to the apartment now?" Ylang Ylang said.

"We should do something with your hair."

"Like what?"

"It needs to be red."

"I like it just the way it is."

"The sun will fall soon."

"Can we go back to the apartment if I let you colour my hair?"

Alice didn't reply, but Ylang Ylang didn't care when she saw the way she smiled. Afterwards, her hair, long and red, wasn't so bad.

"Can we go back to the apartment now?"

"After you see my favourite coffee shop."

Alice asked her right away in the café as Ylang Ylang sipped black coffee and bit into a cheese panini. "Do you like my skin?"

Ylang Ylang loved the way she talked, the sound of her voice. She loved the way her eyes watched intensely; curious orbs of artificial intelligence, seeing more than Ylang Ylang wanted to show. Taking her time, chewing deliberately, she pretended not to care about the question. Alice fell back into the creaking seat, smiling her perception. She already knew the answer, knew Ylang Ylang better than she knew herself. She sipped her wine, but left the aubergine wrap untouched.

Stepping back outside, Alice kissed Ylang Ylang. She tasted of rain and the windswept park, where Alice took her after they finished shopping. Her hands guided Ylang Ylang across her body to the places she wanted to be touched. She pulled open her dress and her teeth rolled Ylang Ylang's nipple. She gasped when Alice bit too hard. Her skin's scent moved Ylang Ylang to the edge, reminded her of the garden in her dreams, the one where she was born as an individual and created by God, not in a lab. The garden where she possessed a soul.

Near curfew, they walked back through the park, following the path that led to the vacant play area. Winter was coming to an end; everyone was sure about that. It hadn't snowed for over a month. Alice lit two cigarettes and handed one to Ylang Ylang, who wondered what pleasure Alice gained from such things. Maybe it was the ritual of lighting the cigarettes that comforted her, she thought. Taking in a final lungful of diluted nicotine, Ylang Ylang stamped the cigarette into the ground and they meandered through the darkness.

A wail. In the distance.

Another. Close by.

More. All around.

Then screams.

Gunshots.

They ran, heading towards the park entrance where they saw sharded racing along the street, rabid and terrifying. Dozens of the violent creatures, grabbing hold of anyone who was not sharded and pulling them apart with their bare hands. Arms, legs, and heads ripped from the screaming residents of York.

More noise.

The growl of numerous motorbikes ridden by sharded creatures streamed into the city.

"We have to get back to the apartment," Alice yelled.

"We won't make it back to the apartment," Ylang Ylang said, pulling Alice into some shrubs near the entrance.

They watched as the sharded smashed their way into buildings, pulled out the occupants, and butchered them. Synthetics, clones, and the few humans that remained in the city. No one was spared.

Flames sprung up all around as the sharded burned everything that would burn. Ylang Ylang turned away when they began to eat the livers pulled from their victims. She could not block out their frenzied howls as they feasted like beasts. Snow started to fall in the windless air, while the sharded continued to run wild through the streets.

"How did they get into the city?" Alice whispered.

Movement behind.

Ylang Ylang turned. A sharded man stared down at them. The right side of his face was normal, human. Fragmented bone and cartilage burst out from his left side. His mouth was normal too, but a second mouth, with an angled jawbone and full set of sharded teeth, grew out of his neck. It gaped open, like it was hungry for something close by.

He spoke through the mouth in his neck. "You smell good," he said to Ylang Ylang. "Do you want to be like me?"

Ylang Ylang squeezed Alice's hand. She was no longer afraid, maybe it was because Alice did not seem afraid anymore. "Why would we ever want to become sharded?" Ylang Ylang asked.

"Not we," he said, "just you."

"It will never stop snowing," Alice said, as she cut her arm with a blade that Ylang Ylang did not realise she carried.

Ylang Ylang knew the truth then, as dark blood dripped from Alice's tubes. Knew the truth about synthetics. Understood why they smoked and drank and sometimes ate. They did it for clones and humans alike, not for themselves. So their living companions would not feel alone. Would not sense the lie they were living.

The engineers of old had their reasons for turning red blood black. They did it to show the darkness at the heart of human nature. "It's so beautiful," Ylang Ylang said, watching the soundless fissile winter fall and land fractal. Seeing the blood turn it black, and realising then, how even in the depths of psychosis, everyone was still so fragile.

"They are not interested in me," Alice said, squeezing her arm to make the blood flow quicker. "I do not have a liver, a soul. But at least we can die together."

"We were never really alive, Alice."

"It doesn't have to be this way," the sharded said to Ylang Ylang.

"What other way is there?" she asked.

"Be like me."

"I will never leave Alice."

Ylang Ylang thought about fighting. It was stupid thinking she could do that. Even with the synthetic strength of Alice to help her, the sharded were much stronger. And this one was so tall and muscular.

As if he knew what was going through Ylang Ylang's head, the sharded man took something from its pocket. A sack. He put the sack over Alice's head. She did not remove it. Pulling the strap from her handbag, he tied it around her arm and the dark fluid that held Alice's synthetic existence together stopped flowing.

The mouth in his neck bit off a small shard from one of his four left arms. He gave the shard to Ylang Ylang.

"What am I supposed to do with this?" she asked.

"Eat it."

"Just like that?"

"Yes."

The howling intensified around them as more sharded entered the city. Gun shots rang out in the distance, but not many. The rumours must have been true about ammunition stores being depleted. Ylang Ylang pulled the shard in half and handed a piece to Alice.

"It won't work on her," the sharded said.

"Can she stay with me, even if she is not sharded?"

He did not speak.

Ylang Ylang gazed at Alice. She did not want to see her dismembered. She knew there was only one way to stop it happening. She put the shard into her mouth and chewed. It was spongy, she didn't expect that, and it tasted of undercooked pork.

She swallowed.

"Eat both pieces," the sharded man said.

She took the other half of shard from Alice and ate it.

Nothing happened.

Then lights flashed inside her head. Darkness. Pain. Her head twisted into a new shape. Then nothing. She opened her eyes. She could not see her head, but she knew it had changed.

"Do you remember anything from your past life?" the sharded man asked

"I remember everything," Ylang Ylang said, in a voice that sounded nothing like her own.

"I don't remember anything," the sharded man said.

"We are all different," a voice inside her head said.

"Who..." Ylang Ylang started to ask.

The sharded man cut in. "He is someone looking out for you, looking out for all of us. He's got our back."

Ylang Ylang lifted the sack off Alice's head.

Alice stared at Ylang Ylang. Her eyes did not show any emotion.

"Show me how I look," Ylang Ylang said to her.

Alice picked her handbag up off the floor and pulled her phone from it. She took a holographic picture of Ylang Ylang and showed it to her.

Ylang Ylang studied herself. Her head was bulbous. She had no lips. Her bottom jaw was elongated and held numerous, sharded teeth. Her once black skin was now textured in colours of red, orange and brown. Small shards of bone and cartilage covered her face, scalp and neck.

"I think you are beautiful," Alice said.

"I do too," Ylang Ylang said, handing the phone back to Alice.

"Can you smell it?" the sharded man asked. "You need to feed on it. Your soul needs to feed."

Ylang Ylang shook her head. "I don't have a soul," she said. "I'm a clone."

"That is a lie," the voice whispered. *"A human lie. Your soul is beautiful, like your friendship with the synthetic."*

Ylang Ylang took hold of Alice's hand. "Take on your true form," she said to her.

Alice frowned. Then smiled. Her head began to change shape. Not in holographic form, like it did earlier. This time, the synthetic materials that made up her head, twisted for real. She looked exactly the same as Ylang Ylang.

"I always wanted to be a twin," Ylang Ylang said, staring at Alice.

"Me too," Alice said. "I don't want to be called Alice now."

"What should I call you?"

"Ylang."

"Call me that name too."

The sharded man stood beside Ylang. He grabbed her other hand and they walked out of the park towards the flames, the howling, and wailing.

"Where are we going?" Ylang asked.

"Paris," the voice in her head replied, *"but first..."*

"The sweet scent of liver." Ylang said.

"Yes."

Nedserd

Dresden 2154

Dorian was the weakest. He was the one William targeted. He could overpower Dorian if he was stronger. William would only get stronger if he could eat more food. That was the conundrum. Like William, the others were starving and the few scraps they were given each day barely delayed their appointments with death. Hunger, real hunger like this, was so painful. Like wasp stings on the brain. It drove William's every thought. That was a lie. The scent drove his every thought. Always on the fringes of his awareness, it called to him like a wasp sting on the soul. It was the inspiration for the idea. He needed to give them something more than a primal urge to fill their stomachs. He needed to give them something that would feed their minds. He needed to give them the meaning of life.

Gunter would be the hardest one to convince. William watched him as he lay on the floor with his head rested on one hand. He used a finger to guide a millipede round and round in circles. He knew William was watching him, just like he knew Josef, Mikhail, Sebastian, and Montana were also watching. All of them waiting for him to pick up the millipede and eat it. William marvelled at Gunter's self-control. How he played with his food that way, when the wasps were doing their thing. Of course, it was a mind game. Everything was in the mind. Gunter had the strongest mind of all of them, but that didn't make him the most devious.

"I overheard Dorian talking to N'Yetsky," William said.

Everyone pretended they weren't listening, but he knew everyone was listening. It was recreation time. They were in the courtyard that was covered with tarpaulin. They never saw the sun. The light beneath the tarpaulin, like everywhere else, was artificial. The wind gusted through the vents in the courtyard, moving the tarpaulin in ripples of spine prickling sound. Sometimes, William heard the tarpaulin ripple even when he wasn't in the courtyard. It must have been something to do with soul.

"Our memories are going to be deleted," William added.

Everyone turned to face him then, except for Gunter. He picked up the millipede, pulled his head back, and dropped it into his gaping mouth. He then faced William, who heard him crunching on the arthropod above the noise of the tarpaulin. The others stared at Gunter as he ate.

Seeing another eat made William envious. Made the wasps sting with greater venom.

"Why would they do that?" Montana finally asked when Gunter finished crunching on the millipede's hard shell. She was always the first to ask the questions everyone else wanted to ask.

"It has something to do with a capacity overload. The servers would soon be at full capacity. Then the system would overload and break down."

"They can't do that," Josef said, "it must be illegal or something."

Josef would probably be the next one to die. He was the weakest.

"They can do whatever they want, any time they want," Mikhail said.

Sebastian leant against the stone wall near the entranceway with his arms crossed. He never looked at anyone when he spoke and right then, he stared at the tarpaulin. "If they do that, we won't know who we used to be or why we agreed to take part in this experiment."

"It must be a lie," Mikhail yelled. "They told us we have a purpose in life. Everything will be revealed at the end. We just need to keep faith and die."

"Then why did they say they were going to erase our memories from the server?" Montana asked.

Mikhail clenched his fists and if his facial nerves had not been incapacitated, then his expression would surely have been one of rage. "We serve a purpose. Erasing our memories from the server is a lie."

Dorian and N'Yetsky had carried out the surgery. They said it was necessary to remove displays of emotion from our faces in order for the experiment to work. It was also the reason we couldn't taste anything.

"Isn't there a Committee of Social Justice we can appeal to?" Josef asked.

Gunter sighed. "Yes, there probably is. No, we probably can't appeal. We are no longer part of society."

"You don't know that for sure," Mikhail said. "You can't possibly remember."

"I don't remember, but look around you, do you really think anyone cares about us?"

Montana bit on what was left of her nails. "Surely they would have killed us already if we were worthless," she said between bites.

"I'm sure you are right, Montana," Josef said.

"We are nothing without our memories," Sebastian said, pushing himself away from the wall. He began to pace the courtyard, with his shoulders slumped and his head down. His thin arms dangled at his side, little more than bone and skin.

"We are already nothing," Gunter said. "Our memories were never going to be returned."

Josef sat up from his lying position. "I still have memories. I can remember the first time I was brought here."

"And you remember nothing before you were brought here, just like the rest of us."

"I keep getting flashes."

"It is nothing more than your mind playing tricks on you."

"What if it isn't my mind playing tricks? What if they are visions?"

"Visions of what?"

"Visions of life after death."

"Is that what you think you see?"

"I see the sun and green fields. Plenty to eat for all. Don't you see them too?"

"Yes, but they are not visions, they are longings."

"There must be more to life than this place," Montana said, "I feel it inside me like I feel hunger."

Gunter shook his head. "There is no meaning to life, other than it being a conduit to death."

Sebastian no longer had the energy to walk. He sat down a few yards from our circle and rubbed his head. "If that is true, then why do we cling onto life when we are starving like this? Why don't we stop eating and simply die?"

"I can't answer that, Sebastian," William said. "All I know is that we need our memories returning. It's the only way to know for sure our purpose in life and I think I know how we can make that happen."

"What have you got planned?" Montana asked.

"If I could overpower a guard, I could get him to take us to the control room, force him to give us back our memories. Then we would know why we are here. Then we would know the meaning of life."

"You are too weak," Gunter said. "You could never do that."

William drew a circle in the dirt with his finger, then retraced the circle several times. "I could if I had enough food. I could grow strong. Dorian is weaker than N'Yetsky. I could overpower him."

"Where are you going to get enough food to do that?" Josef asked.

"I don't know," he lied, "it was just a thought."

He knew how he could get enough food, but he didn't want to be the one to say it. If one of the others made the suggestion, there would be more chance of them doing what he wanted.

"A stupid thought," Gunter said.

"There is a way," Josef said. "There is enough food to make one of us strong."

"How?" Mikhail asked.

"We could give our food to William."

"All of it?" Montana said.

"Not all of it. Say, we give him a quarter or a fifth of our food. That would work."

"No one gets their dirty hands on my food," Gunter said.

"We don't have enough food as it is, if we lose even a fifth of it…" Mikhail never finished what he was going to say.

"Don't you want to know why you are here before you die?" Sebastian asked. "Or if you have a family outside of Rethguals?"

"I only want to eat," Gunter said.

"Do you really think you could overpower Dorian?" Montana asked me.

"Yes," I replied.

"I don't think I can get any hungrier," Montana said. "You can have a share of my food."

"She is going to feed you her toenails," Gunter said.

Sebastian threw a stone at Gunter then looked up towards the tarpaulin. "I will give you a small portion of my food each day. Do not let us down, William, we are trusting you with more than our food."

William waited a suitable time before replying. "I know, Sebastian. I know."

"You can have all of my food," Josef said.

The bell suddenly rang, and their discussion ended as they silently made their way from the courtyard to the washroom. After they applied face cream, they each drank a cup of water and settled down to sleep for the night.

The next morning, William wasn't thinking straight. No one who is starving ever thinks straight. If he had been thinking, he would never have eaten all the food Josef offered him. That was dumb. Josef died that night, and the overseers took him away the next morning. William had lost any future share in his food. Still, there was a positive side to things. Josef died in his sleep before they downloaded his memories. It was confirmation that William spoke the truth about their memories being deleted.

Mikhail must have realised William told the truth. He gave William a fifth of his food when they next ate. Only Gunter held back, and he only held back for two days. Then, he crumbled like the rest and begrudgingly handed over a portion of his food. Even the strongest mind has its limitations. Everyone wants to belong to something. He gave William less food than the others, but it was more than he expected.

As each day passed, and William became stronger, his hunger remained extreme. He constantly craved food, or was it something else? Something to do with the scent. Its source was deep within the facility, a place he had never been. It shifted around like it was moving, as if the scent had legs. If William ever escaped, the first place he would go would be the source of the scent.

Watching his fellow prisoners become weaker was difficult. William tried to put it from his mind. It was easy putting their welfare from his mind. After the first few days of sharing their food with William, they stopped talking to him. They still talked to each other, but whenever he approached the circle in the courtyard where most discussions occurred, they would go silent. It was odd how they would share their food with him, but not their thoughts.

Each to his own seemed to be the new world order.

It was different with Dorian. He seemed more interested in William than ever before as he examined the skin on his face and took extra blood and urine samples. If he suspected that William was eating more than his fair share of food, he did not mention it. There were rarely any overseers in the refectory to notice how things had changed.

"Josef died before you downloaded his memories into his brain," William said. "We will never get to know who we were before we die, will we?"

Dorian didn't answer. The overseers seldom answered questions. William wondered if they were programmed not to answer, or if it was something about their psyche that made them nonresponsive. He wanted to know if it was possible for a synthetic to disobey a program. He pushed the jar of cream off the arm of the chair. It landed on the floor, breaking into fragments of cream covered glass. Dorian left his side and started to clean up the mess. His arms looked as thin as William's, but where his were skin and bone, Dorian's arms were synthetic skin and mechanical rods. The synthetic's skin was so smooth, with no shards sticking out from anywhere. Why didn't they make automatons look like humans? Why did they make them look like skeletons? It probably had something to do with finances. He overheard N'Yetsky say finances were tight. There was never enough money.

"I want to make a complaint to the Committee of Social Injustice," William said.

Dorian continued to clean up the mess, as if he hadn't heard the request.

William stood up and made to leave the examination room. When he reached the door and opened it, Dorian took notice and strode towards him.

"Please sit back down, William," he said in a friendly voice, grabbing his arm and pulling him back towards the seat in an unfriendly manner.

William attempted to pull his arm from Dorian's grasp, but he squeezed more firmly. William yelled out in pain as the pressure almost crushed his arm.

"Please," Dorian said, indicating for him to sit in the chair.

Dorian was too strong. William realised he had no choice but to do as he asked. He was always going to be too powerful for him, even with the extra food portions William was eating. It was something he had known from the first time he had the idea.

He was so hungry, he didn't care.

Dorian got another jar of cream from the cupboard and applied it to his face. William closed his eyes and focused on the sound of tarpaulin moving in the wind. It didn't chase away the wasps completely, but it did subdue them a little.

"Whose orders do you follow, Dorian?" he asked.

Dorian surprised him by answering, "I follow only the Grand Overseer's instructions," he said.

"Who is the Grand Overseer?"

"He is the one in charge."

"In charge of the control room?"

"In charge of everything."

William tried to get more out of Dorian regarding the Grand Overseer, but he wouldn't say anymore. When he finished applying the cream, he escorted him back to his room. William sat on his bed and picked up the book he was reading, about an old man, alone in a small boat at sea, fishing for marlin. Before he got his catch back to land, his catch was eaten by sharks. All the sharks left were the marlin's heads. William could understand the sharks' hunger. He could understand their pain. The book affected him deeply. He couldn't decide if it was his new favourite book, or if The Three Musketeers was still his favourite. He decided to read them both again before he made up his mind.

The food they were allocated each day never changed. They all received one slice of bread and one bowl of broth. The vending machine was located next to the entrance inside the refectory. At mid-day, each day, William stood in front of the eye recognition unit and his daily serving was duly dispensed. The others followed his lead and before they took their seats, they would pass by and hand over a portion of their food to him. Mikhail gave him exactly six level spoonful's of his broth and a fifth of his bread, which he measured using the top half of his thumb that just happened to be a fifth of the length of the bread. The others haphazardly spooned their portions into his bowl and broke off an approximate amount of their bread, apart from Gunter. He gave him his share of broth, but not his bread.

He never explained why.

Once they started to share their food, the seating arrangements changed. William sat on his own, while Gunter, Mikhail and Montana sat at the opposite end of the refectory. Sebastian, who normally sat alone, now joined the others. Josef's seat was always pulled out from the table as if he, too, sat with them. William's old seat remained pushed underneath the table. They only ever spoke to him about one thing and it was always Montana who asked.

"When are you going to be strong enough?" she said as she handed over her portion of food.

"Now that Josef has died," he said, "and I am eating less food, it will take a little longer."

"How much longer?" she asked.

"A fifth longer. Unless I receive more food."

The very next morning, the food they gave him increased.

William was surprised when Gunter became the next one to die. He always thought Gunter was the strongest. When Mikhail died a few days later, he was not surprised. Neither one of them were taken away before they died. Their memories were not downloaded into their brains. Prior to Josef dying, he couldn't remember anyone ever dying in Rethguals. Dorian and N'Yetsky were supposed to monitor their health and take them to the control room just before they died so their memories could be downloaded and the reason for their suffering would be revealed. It seemed the conversation he overheard was true, their memories had been deleted.

"Are you strong enough yet?" Montana asked the day Mikhail died.

"No," he replied, "and now that I am getting less food, it will take longer. Maybe you and Sebastian should give me more of your portion. We don't have much time left."

They must have talked while he was sleeping. The next time

William ate, they gave him half of their food portion. It's frightening how quickly the body wastes away when it is not fed enough food. Both Sebastian and Montana were little more than stick people now. He stared down at his arms. He couldn't remember them ever looking so full, yet his stomach had shrunk, even though he was feeding it more. Sebastian and Montana's stomachs looked bloated. Maybe it was an illusion, due to the rest of their bodies being so thin. Wait, perhaps they had found a secret stash of food they were hiding from him.

He decided he needed to watch them more closely.

If they had a secret stash of food, he never found it. Montana only lasted three more days before she died. Dorian took her away and it was no surprise to see that her memories were not downloaded prior to her death. Before Sebastian died, William managed to eat all his food for two more days. He was too weak to argue. He let William do whatever he wanted. They carried him from the courtyard on a stretcher and when William shouted about his memories, they didn't even look his way.

The next day was difficult, eating just one portion of food was nightmarishly painful for William. He forgot what real hunger was until the wasps began to chew on his brain as well as sting. He needed a different plan, something that would get him into the control room. He decided his only option was to die. He wanted to wait until the next day before he died, so he at least got one more meal to eat, but the wasps would not wait another day.

When it was time for him to enter the courtyard, William caught two millipedes and ate them while he thought about what to do. Since Gunter died, millipedes had become much easier to find. After eating, he lay down and closed his eyes, waiting for the bell to sound. It took a few moments after the bell pealed before one of the automatons entered the courtyard. William was pleased when he heard N'Yetsky's feet scrape across the concrete floor. He always dragged his feet, unlike Dorian, who always lifted his feet like he was walking on hot coals. As N'Yetsky approached, William stopped breathing. There must have been some form of sensor on the palm of the synthetic's hand. Each time there was a death, one of the automatons would place the palm of its hand above the mouth of the suspected deceased. N'Yetsky was clumsy and not as methodical as Dorian.

It would be easier to fool him.

"Is William dead?" Dorian said as he entered the courtyard.

"He's not breathing," N'Yetsky responded.

"What about a heartbeat?"

N'Yetsky sighed, "He is not breathing. Grab hold of his legs. We need to get him out of here and prepare for the new arrivals."

As they carried William out of the courtyard, he tried to keep his breathing as shallow as possible. N'Yetsky stopped at the door that led to the control room and must have placed his synthetic eyes against the recognition unit because William heard the door click open. The air immediately felt different as they carried him through the opening. It was cooler and smelled pleasant. He never realised how bad prison smelled until he left it behind. The top half of his body, where N'Yetsky held onto him, was roughly dropped onto a hard surface and he almost opened his eyes in shock. Dorian gently lowered his legs and William remained as still as he was able to.

"I will go and awaken them," N'Yetsky said.

William heard another door open and N'Yetsky leave. Then, he heard Dorian sit down. He opened his eyes into slits and saw that he had been placed on a table in the centre of the room. Dorian sat in front of a monitor to the left of William. The control room was perfectly white and the glare from the overhead lights was almost too bright, making everything appear to blur into everything else. He closed his eyes and slowly opened them again, hoping they would become accustomed to this new, odd light.

Everything still appeared blurred.

The monitor was different, the image there was perfectly sharp. He saw N'Yetsky on the monitor, looking up at the camera in the room where he stood.

"I will bring them to the control room now," N'Yetsky's tinny voice said through a speaker.

N'Yetsky disappeared from view. Dorian moved a joystick and another room appeared on the monitor where N'Yetsky was now located. William almost gasped in shock when he saw eleven operating tables in the room. On each table lay a person he knew. Edgar, Yon, Wild Bob, Isaac, and Valencia.

The first five to die.

They were positioned alongside Josef, Gunter, Mikhail, Montana, Sebastian, and William.

"The new arrivals have all been operated on and their memories have been downloaded," N'Yetsky said. "I'm about to administer the anti-anaesthetic now."

"Very well," Dorian replied. "I will meet you in the courtyard. Once they are fully awake, bring them and we can begin the indoctrination."

Dorian got up and William quickly closed his eyes. Despite trying to remain as still as he possibly could, his heart raced wildly. The door clicked open, and Dorian left the control room, closing the door behind him.

William immediately opened his eyes and sat up, retching. He wasn't sick. The stomach cramps were incredibly painful. Standing, ignoring the pain, he walked over to the monitor. Dorian stood motionless in the courtyard. That was not what William was interested in, though. He flicked the joystick until the room with the new arrivals appeared. They were now sitting up on the operating tables. He stared at his double, feeling both perplexed and creeped out. Like the others, his double looked straight ahead as if it didn't see what was directly in front of it.

As if it didn't see anything at all.

"Follow me," N'Yetsky said, turning his back on them and heading for the doorway. The new arrivals slid down from the operating tables and followed N'Yetsky in single file. William flicked the joystick and watched on the monitor as they moved down a long corridor, until they approached the control room. Then, he dashed back to the table and lay down with his eyes closed.

The door to the control room opened and he heard them file past until N'Yetsky stopped, opened the door the opposite that led to the courtyard and exited.

William opened his eyes and noticed, for the first time, the sign above the courtyard door. It read *House Five.* He did not know its meaning. Sitting up, he saw that N'Yetsky had left the other door open. He stared at the opening for a moment, then glanced over at the monitor as the new arrivals lined up in front of N'Yetsky and Dorian.

"It is time to activate them," Dorian said.

N'Yetsky nodded a response and they both stood in front of one of the new arrivals. They raised a hand and held it in front of the clone. The palms of their hands began to flash and a moment later, the two clones looked around the courtyard with a bemused expression on their faces. The synthetics repeated the process with the others.

"May I have your attention?" Dorian said. "I know you all must be feeling disorientated, but it will soon pass. For now, know that you are all here for a special purpose, one which you all agreed to complete."

William recognised the speech and remembered how, over the next few days, they would be told about their memories being stored safely, how they would be returned once the experiment was completed. They would be informed that Rethguals was a medical research centre. Later, they would discover the truth and understand that it was, in fact, a penitentiary.

Moving away from the monitors, William walked over to the open door and stepped through it. He stood inside a long corridor with doors left and right. He knew where to go next. The scent that tormented his soul was incredibly strong in this place. It led to a door at the far end of the corridor.

The door opened and a creature he had never seen before

stepped into view. It almost looked like a synthetic, and almost looked human, like William. But it was neither. Its skin was too wrinkled to be a synthetic and there were no shards protruding from its face like William's. He did not know what to call it.

The scent came from the creature.

It waved at him. "William, come here," it said. "Now is the time for you to learn the truth."

He knew it was lying. There was no truth in Rethguals. William walked towards the creature anyway. He had nowhere else to go.

"My name is Truk Tugennov," the creature said, gesturing for William to follow it through the doorway.

The doorway led into a room filled with things William had never seen before. Where he knew only white walls and concrete flooring, Tugennov's room had deep red walls and a dark wooden floor. It was lavishly furnished with ornate seating and soft fabric coverings. The whole space was full of paintings, curios, and ornaments stacked on every possible surface.

All William could focus on, though, was the scent coming from Tugennov. Deep within his body, the scent was strongest. The wasp stings frenzied William's brain as the creature's scent aroused his very essence.

"It's been a while since we last talked," Tugennov said, closing the door. "Please, sit down, William."

William looked around for a suitable place to sit and spotted the edge of a couch that did not have something stored upon it. Tugennov sat on a chair, by a desk with a monitor on top of it, directly opposite to where he sat.

"We've talked before?" William asked, not remembering ever having done so.

"Not exactly me and you. I have talked to a clone of you."

Tugennov's words sank in and William knew, at last, he was listening to the truth.

"We never had any memories, did we?"

"No."

"Why did you lie to us about that?"

"Everyone needs a reason to live. Even clones. Faith in a good cause, and the books we allow you to read, seem to be enough to keep you going for the length of time you are useful to us."

William wanted to hit Tugennov after hearing him say those words. More so, he wanted to know about the meaning of life. Wanted to know his purpose in the grand scheme. "Tell me about Rethguals and why you kept us prisoners here."

"Rethguals is an experimentation centre."

"You are lying."

"I have no reason to lie."

"Rethguals is a prison full of contradictions and lies."

"I can see how you would see it that way."

"What other way is there to see it?"

"I already told you. This is an experimentation facility. We are looking for a cure to the contagion."

"Huh?"

"Forgive me, I forgot you have no memories of that part of history. The contagion started in a small English town called Darlington, many years ago. It quickly spread, infecting millions around the world. It almost wiped out humanity. We fought against the infected and are currently at an impasse, with neither side able to overpower the other."

A story William read came to his mind, *Never Let Me Go*. The story upset him, but he enjoyed reading it. "Who did you clone me from?" he asked. "Was his name William? Did he have any children?"

William wanted to ask if he had a soul.

Tugennov stared at him for a short moment. "William," he finally said, "you are not a human clone, you are a clone of the sharded."

His words sank in.

Tugennov was the human. He was... what was he?

Sharded.

He looked up at his reflection in the mirror screwed to the ceiling.

His beautiful, sharded face had never looked so healthy. The extra food portions had done wonders. Staring across at Tugennov, he felt sorry for him. He looked so ugly but smelled so good.

"Why is your face lined and not smooth like a synthetic?"

Tugennov laughed. "It's an age thing, William. I used to have skin as smooth as a synthetic's, but I'm seventy-three years old now. Time is not kind to humans."

"How old am I?"

"You are two months old."

He didn't feel that young. It felt like he should be older than Tugennov. Over a hundred years old.

"What is my purpose in life?"

"In the other houses, we are attempting to develop an airborne virus that attacks the skin of the sharded. The experiments have not been going well. In House Five, we put the virus in the cream we apply to your skin. Initial trials proved very successful, but the sharded are an amazingly adaptable species. We haven't managed to develop a virus that can transmute quick enough to outpace your ability to become immune after the initial virus wave kills off a few thousand of you. We never managed to kill a single sharded from your group. I'm sure we will get there eventually, though."

It didn't make sense. They didn't need conscious subjects to perform the experiments.

"You don't need to ask your next question," Tugennov said, smiling. "I already know what it is. We wouldn't be able to do a behaviour study if we kept you unconscious. We need to learn what makes you tick. If the virus is a failure, we may identify another weakness by observing you. It's not very scientific, in truth. Being clones, you don't have all the history of your kind to bring to mind. You don't feel the need to eat human livers like your infected cousins in the wild."

Eat human liver.

That scent.

"And of course," Tugennov continued, "we must perform surgery to remove your aggressive behaviour. We do that by removing part of the amygdala region from your brains."

William had no idea what Tugennov was talking about. He just wanted to kill him. Before he did, he wanted to know more about everything in general.

"Your actions are inhuman. You are like a shark who sees me as a marlin."

Tugennov shrugged. "You do and say the same things every time, you know. It's fascinating to me, how things are repeated."

"What do you mean?"

"You always convince the others to give you their food."

I couldn't stop staring at my beautiful face in the mirror.

"How many times have I convinced the others?"

"You are William 82."

William thought he should have been disgusted with himself, but Tugennov's words did not upset him.

Tugennov continued. "You always follow the same path afterwards and pretend to be dead. Of course, we go along with your game, until you sit here with me like this now, talking this talk. It absolutely perplexes me."

"Why?"

"Because it shouldn't happen the same way every time, yet it continues to do so. Nothing is repeatable this way. It troubles me. One of these days you must do something different. I am waiting for that day. I am waiting for you to come up with a different question, at least. Or for one of the others to see through you and to eat your food instead. When that happens, I can relax."

"Why can't you relax until then?"

"Because I'm questioning if this is really happening to me or if I am stuck inside some kind of *Groundhog Day* that stretches into infinity where the ending is always the same."

"How do things usually end?"

"With you asking me that exact question."

"And then what?"

"Then I press this," he pointed to a switch on the desk, "and Dorian takes you to the processor."

"The processor?"

"Yes, the food processor. We can't afford to waste your flesh and bones, even what little there is of it. You and the others are processed into clone broth. That's what we feed you each day."

"What if I stop you calling Dorian?"

"You always try to stop me, but you never succeed. You are too weak."

"I have been eating more food. I am stronger."

"You are not strong enough."

He studied Tugennov's face. Something suddenly struck him. "How long have you been carrying out these experiments?"

"More years than I care to remember."

"Then something has changed. You are a lot older than when you first had this conversation with William number one."

"Yes."

"You are weaker."

Tugennov's expression changed, his skin wrinkled even more than it already did. Maybe he had finally asked a different question. Tugennov made a move to press the call switch on the desk.

William also moved and grabbed Tugennov's arm before he pressed the switch. "It seems you are also slower," he said.

Tugennov attempted to wrench his arm from William's grasp. He almost managed to free himself, but William was marginally stronger. Feeling the fight could go either way, William decided to act fast. He pushed Tugennov onto the floor and kicked him in the stomach.

William liked hearing him gasp in pain.

He sat on Tugennov's chest and waited for him to tire as he struggled to get free.

"A synthetic never disobeys a program," William said when Tugennov stopped moving. "Does it disobey an order?"

"What do you mean?" Tugennov managed to say, wheezing heavily.

"If I order Dorian to take you to the food processor, would he do as I command?"

"Don't be absurd, Dorian only takes orders from me."

"What if you are dead?"

Tugennov tried to push William off him. It was a wasted effort. William stood and used his foot to keep Tugennov on the ground. He looked around for something to hit him with. A pair of wooden clogs with hinged heels stood on the desk. William picked one up. It felt weighty in his hand. He hit Tugennov over the head with it. Tugennov shrieked. William hit him again and Tugennov covered his head with his arms. It was more difficult to connect with his head now that his arms were in the way, but William continued to strike with the clog until Tugennov's eyes closed and he stopped moving.

He still breathed.

William moved Tugennov's arms to the side and hit him until he stopped breathing and his head was covered in blood. He remembered what Dorian said to N'Yetsky about checking for a heartbeat. He checked Tugennov's pulse. There was no pulse. Killing someone that way was more humane than starving them to death, he was sure of it.

He pulled at Tugennov's jaw, stretching it a few inches from his face. When he dropped the jaw, it did not spring back into place. Tugennov almost looked sharded with his jaw elongated that way. He prodded one of the dead eyes, then pulled it out from its socket. Pressing it between his fingers, the eyeball returned to its normal shape when he released the pressure. He left loose of it, and it hung half in, half out, of the eye socket.

The sweet scent waned a little. That was not a good thing. William pulled open Tugennov's clothing. The scent came from beneath his skin. It was at its most pungent just below his right ribcage. Using his hands and teeth, William ripped at Tugennov's flesh until he got to the source of the aroma that had been driving him crazy as long as he could remember.

Liver.

It glistened in his hands.

He sank his teeth into the organ. That first taste of human liver... Oh, how the taste almost usurped the scent as his favourite thing ever. Blood dripped down his chin and fell onto his chest. William could not stop himself from gorging until he consumed every last ounce of Tugennov's liver. For the first time in his young life, the wasps did not sting his brain. Hunger was replaced with the beating wings of a thousand wasps as they caressed his soul. There was more. He felt something else. A presence. Not a physical presence, it was spiritual in nature.

"I mean you no harm."

William stared down at Tugennov's face.

"I will stay with you forever."

The voice came from Tugennov's dead mouth, which uttered more words. *"A father to your soul."*

"Who are you?"

Tugennov's body sat up and its dead eyes stared at William. *"Scientific studies completed over the years with worms have attempted to prove that memories can be transferred from one worm to another when one worm eats another. The studies never proved conclusive. That's because the scientists who carried out the studies didn't do them correctly. If a man ate my flesh, not only would my superior senses be transferred to the man, but so too would my exquisite sharded form. And the best thing is, he would never age."*

"Are you saying I am going to turn into you because I ate your liver?"

"You didn't eat my liver. You ate Tugennov's liver. His soul is now

yours, not mine. Yet, you are still me because you were cloned from someone who was sharded like me."

"I don't have superior senses."

"They will return once the drugs wear off. Just make sure you don't swallow any more medications. You are so much more than your captors and you have the means to turn the tables on them. You must be patient, though, and wait for me to return in my true form before you unleash your army."

"My army?"

The presence stopped speaking and Tugennov's body slumped to the floor. William kicked the body, but it did not respond. He was unsure what to do next. The presence was still with him. In the background, like it was sleeping. Sitting in the seat where Tugennov had sat earlier, he pressed the switch and waited. A gentle knock at the door sounded a moment later.

"Come in," William said.

The door opened slowly and Dorian entered the room. He looked at William, then at Tugennov on the floor. William could almost hear Dorian's programs turning over inside his central processing unit as he decided what to do next.

"Mr Tugennov is dead," William said.

Dorian did not respond.

"Do you understand, Dorian?"

"Yes."

"Before he died, he put me in charge. I am now the Grand Overseer of Rethguals. Do you understand?"

"Yes."

"How many clones do we have in storage?"

"Do I call you William or Grand Overseer?"

"Call me William. How many clones do we have in storage?"

"Not as many as in the past. Some have been sent to other research facilities."

"That's not what I asked."

"There are one hundred and fifty thousand clones in the refrigeration facility, give or take a few hundred."

William smiled. "We have an army to train and command, Dorian. Me, you, and William 83 need to become the three musketeers of Rethguals."

Dorian cocked his head. "Don't you mean the four musketeers of Rethguals?"

"No, I mean the three musketeers. Okay?"

"Yes."

"Good. Now I want you to take Mr Tugennov's remains to the food processor. Do not feed his remains to the clones. Once he has been processed, bring a sample of him back to me. Do you understand, Dorian?"

"Yes."

"You can take Mr Tugennov away now."

Dorian bent down and lifted Tugennov from the floor, then left the room, carefully closing the door behind him.

William felt no satisfaction being the new Grand Overseer of Rethguals. Right at that moment, all he felt was hunger and the utmost need to stop the wasps stinging his brain. And finally, he knew exactly how to stop the stinging.

Gleb

Paris 2154

No one knew Zelda like Gleb. He knew she was different to how the masses viewed her. She once said that she had never seen an ugly bridge before. Gleb felt exactly the same way. He couldn't understand why people were so stupid. Why they didn't realise you could never touch another's soul. It was difficult enough trying to touch your own. He looked down from Pont Neuf at the languid water below as it flowed to Le Harve. He wished he could flow as gracefully. He would join Zelda, if only he could find the courage to jump. If only he wasn't terrified of her ever seeing him as ugly. He was relieved to see his reflection distorted in the murkiness below. He could still see his eyes were out of align, though and that his left eye was much larger than his right. His lopsided mouth and crooked teeth were visible too. And his chin, so long and narrow, it was the one feature of his face he hated the most. At least he did not have shards sprouting out of his face. His life would be much worse if they thought he was sharded rather than just a mutated freak. What everyone thought of him did not matter. All that mattered was how Zelda saw him.

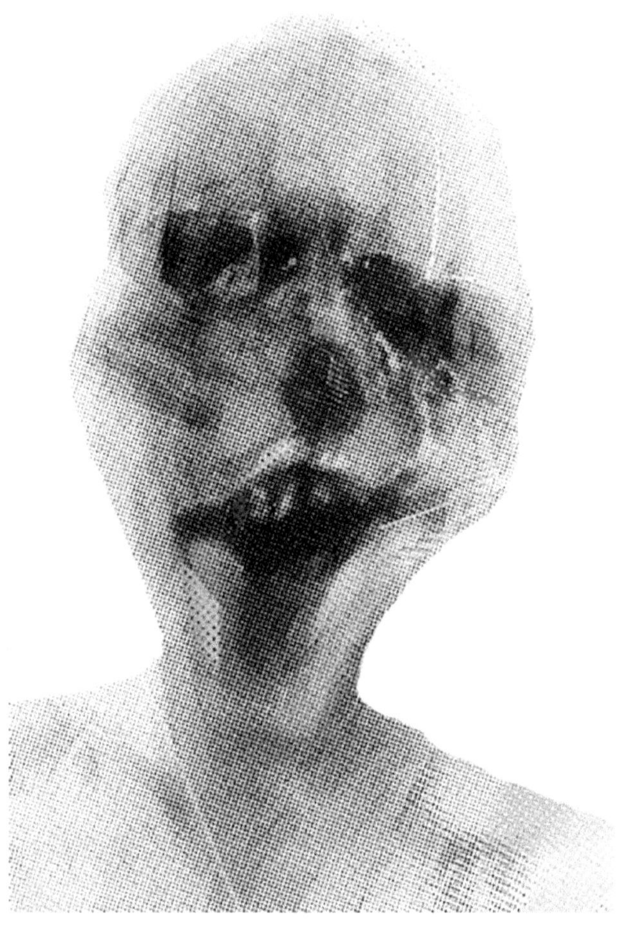

Thirty-seven bridges spanned the Seine in Paris, and he visited each one every thirty-seven days, hoping to bridge the dead air between himself and Zelda. The oldest bridge, ironically named Pont Neuf, was his favourite. He always felt closest to Zelda here, more so than on any other bridge. It had something to do with the air in this particular place, how peaceful it felt in the night to morning transition, just before the city of light fully awakened.

Zelda died on the 4th August in 1962. Gleb was born on the 4th August. Too many years after she died for him to have ever known her. He didn't know for sure if her death and his birth were perfectly synchronised, but he felt inside that it must have been that way. Gleb never met Zelda until he was twenty three, when he saw her picture in the movie theatre. She lay there, discarded like a used tissue, yet her grace remained intact. And her eyes, how they cared for Gleb, held so much life. He picked up the picture and wiped it clean. Always, it remained close to him.

He never watched any of her movies, not even The Misfits, which was the only movie he was tempted to see, purely because of the title. He never watched any movies. Movies were the mana of the perverted who twisted beauty and turned it into something else entirely, something celluloid in nature.

He digested everything about her he could find. Pictures, books, interviews, newspaper articles, and documentaries. He loved to listen to her voice when she spoke in interviews. That's how he discovered she changed her name to Zelda Zonk whenever she stayed in a hotel and wanted to remain anonymous. After each word he read about Zelda, he felt a little closer to her soul. Like him, she had been brought up in foster homes. Unlike him, she transcended. Although she lived in a world where every morning she woke up beautiful, it was enough for Gleb to know she thought in the same way he did. Her mind, like her eyes, was filled with beauty. Not today, though. Today, the news report confirmed something he had been anxious about for some time. He was certain it was not Zelda's fault. She had merely been a pawn to be used and abused by the masses. Always, it was this way with beauty. Always, they destroyed beauty.

He scanned the holopad, careful not to read the headline he knew so well.

A 15-minute film of a movie star engaging in oral sex with an unidentified man will be kept from public view by a New York busi-nessman who has bought it for 1.5 billion credits.

Never had anything affected him so profoundly as that disclosure. Not since he discovered Zelda had died all those years ago, before he was even born. How infinitely cruel his imagination could twist his thoughts. Still, every day, he would thank the unidentified businessman for keeping the film from the public's eyes. If it ever found its way into Gleb's hands, he would burn it in an instant. He dropped the red leaf he had picked up in the park and watched it fall back and forth until it sank into the dark water below.

How easy it would be to fall like a leaf.

"Worry not, Zelda," Gleb said, "we can talk about this later. For now, it is too painful for me to contemplate. Know that I do not blame you, though."

Stepping off the bridge and breaking his connection with Zelda was always difficult, but Gleb had no choice. If he remained any longer, he would be late for work. Ensuring the hood covered his face, he walked along Rue Dauphine with his left foot dragging against the pavement. Ignoring the sounds of the city, he focused his mind on the water as it echoed in the space beneath the bridge. He could always bring that sound to mind, even in the most distressing of times, even when he thought about wordless secrets. He suddenly remembered it was his birthday. How could he forget? He pulled the photo from his breast pocket and stared at her. It was a black and white image, the edges darkened into nothing. He could never make up his mind for sure, but it looked like Zelda was leaning against a window. She held a cigarette delicately between her index and middle finger while the tip of her thumb touched her ring finger like it needed to feel some-thing familiar. She smiled with her mouth closed and her eyes atten-tive. A man stood in front of her. Only the side of his head and his blurred hands were visible. In Gleb's mind, he was the blurred man in the picture and Zelda's eyes wanted to look at no other man but him.

"Everything of importance is held inside your head," Gleb's

mother once told him. *"There is no reality other than what you choose to keep alive inside your mind."*

He believed every word she said that day.

Before he reached Rue Di Buci, the anti-gravity truck carrying the sharded labourers breezed past and Gleb knew he was late. He couldn't walk any faster, so he put the photo back in his pocket and thought about the excuse he was going to make today. He needed to be more disciplined; he couldn't afford to lose this job. He'd never find another. His mother had told him to be strong, that final day. Ignore hurtful words and look only for the good in every bad situation because it was going to be impossible for him to avoid bad situations. He had always tried to do that, but it was getting more difficult as each day passed and his body grew less controllable. There was some good in his job, it meant he could walk to work while it was dark and walk home after work when it was dark again.

At the crossroad he saw the theatre door up ahead. It looked the same as any of the other entrances to the apartment blocks in the street, but it wasn't. Théâtre Xero was known only to a few select people. No tourists ever passed its entranceway.

Victor was waiting by the counter. "You're late again, Gleb."

"It's my birthday."

"You celebrate your birthday?"

"Sometimes."

"You are too ugly to celebrate a birthday. What? You never look in the mirror? You make the sharded look beautiful. Fuck, are you certain your mother wasn't sharded?"

Apart from his reflection in the river, Gleb only ever looked at himself in his apartment mirror. The mirror was serrated and distorted his face. Made it look like he was wearing glasses, even though he was not. For anyone else, the mirror would make them look worse, but for Gleb, he thought it made him look better. Made him look less sharded. Gleb was used to the sharded comparison. Everyone who saw him thought the same. It was why he had to keep his face hidden within a hood whenever he went outside. It was more important to keep his neck concealed. If they saw his neck, they would know for sure he was sharded.

He walked towards the storeroom and opened the door.

"Look at your leg," Victor continued, "your arm and that fucking ugly hump on your back. Shit, and your face. Forget about birthdays and turn up for work on time."

"It won't happen again."

Gleb pulled the cleaning trolley from the storeroom, grateful he could rest his weight against it.

"If it happens again, don't bother turning up. There are plenty more retards who would work for free just to be given the opportunity to do your job. Who else do you think, but a fool like me, would hire a cripple like you to clean up after them?"

"Sorry, Victor," Gleb said, as he filled the bucket with cleaning fluid.

Victor moved towards him. "Forget sorry. Go and do your job and make sure you work an extra hour to make up your time."

He whipped Gleb across the back with the riding crop he always carried.

Gleb flinched, knowing from past experience it was a mistake to appear unaffected by the cruelty his boss inflicted.

Victor returned to the counter muttering to himself, while Gleb walked over to the first cubicle and stepped inside. A single wooden chair was positioned in front of the holographic-screen. Underneath the screen, the carnal droid quietly hissed. One of the seals on the vacuum pump needed repairing. A customer must have been too forceful the previous night when he inserted his penis into the opening. It would have looked just like a mouth once a credit had been paid. The customer was free to choose whichever imaginary person he wanted to use and abuse. The carnal droid was installed with holographic technology and images of over a thousand men and women. It was even possible for the customer to upload a picture of their own choosing and have that displayed on the carnal droid, be it a celebrity, a work colleague, or neighbour. The choice was infinite.

Next to the chair stood a metal bin, and on the shelf beside it, sat a box of tissues. With some difficulty, Gleb bent down and gathered the used tissues off the floor. Just as he reached the last of the them, the thin aroma of semen reached his senses. Forcing back the gag reflex, he stood up and began to mop the floor. It always dumbfounded him how the genesis of a soul could smell so foul. Each day, he understood with greater clarity why Zelda had left everything behind. He didn't believe the conspiracy theories. He knew Zelda had taken her own life and also the reason why she had done so. With each individual sperm he mopped up off the floor, he couldn't help but think that he was cleaning up the seed of another broken soul. Wiping the holo-screen clean, he hoped there were other ephemeral souls in the world like him and Zelda. Souls whose voices would echo in the still air beneath an arched bridge. It was his thirty-seventh birthday today and he wondered about the process of a soul breaking away from a body. He wondered again about Zelda and if she would ever find him ugly.

Of course she would.

After he finished his cleaning duties, he made Victor a coffee and took it to him at the counter.

"I told you already," Victor said to a small man standing opposite him at the counter, "I don't know your sister."

"You don't know where she is?" the man said.

"That's what I said."

Gleb placed the coffee cup on the counter and the man stared at him without balking, crossing his chest with his fingers, or worse still, looking pitiful. Gleb liked him already.

"Get back inside," Victor shouted at Gleb. "What have I told you about staying out of sight of the customers!"

Gleb turned around and headed back towards the curtain leading to the booths.

"I'm not a fucking customer," the small man yelled before Gleb ducked beneath the curtain.

Business was slow; it had been slow for weeks. Gleb could understand Victor's anxiety. He could understand his need to vent his frustration. Gleb was the only one he could rage against. He forgave Victor.

Freak was different. He didn't like Victor. He would never forgive him. Gleb worried about Freak. He worried about what he was capable of doing. It was time to feed Freak.

Walking with his left foot dragging against the floor, Gleb entered the kitchen and got his lunch out of the fridge. Exiting, he made his way towards the last booth and stopped outside. He listened for a short while and when satisfied that Victor was still in the main reception area, he entered the booth and sat down on the floor behind the chair. He gently knocked on the wooden panel and, immediately, there was an identical knock from the other side of the panel.

Gleb removed the loose screw from the panel, pressed it in just the right place and smiled as it opened inwards. No one else knew about the space behind the panel, just Gleb and Freak. Opening the baguette wrapper, Gleb placed the baguette on the floor. Freak picked it up and Gleb listened as his friend ate.

"Sundays are the loneliest for me," Gleb said as Freak ate. "Are Sundays the loneliest days for you too?"

He did not wait for Freak to reply.

Freak never spoke.

"I'm going to the railway station after work." It was a lie. Gleb had never been to the railway station. Crowds weren't good for him. He wasn't good for crowds. Talking about doing it comforted him.

"Have you ever been to the station?"

Gleb had only seen Freak on one occasion, when he caught a glimpse of his reflection in the holo-screen. People would think Freak was ugly like Gleb. They would be frightened of the shards coming out of his neck if they saw them. He understood why he kept out of sight. Gleb didn't flinch when he saw his reflection. He didn't feel any pity. He just wanted to feed Freak.

Zelda said you can learn a lot by watching people. I think I was one of those she talked about at Union Station, one of those who taught her Sunday School, just by how they behaved when she observed them. She would watch as we came and went from the station, see our faces light up when we saw each other again. The young, the old, and the poor, carrying bundles of ragged clothes and emotionally dependant kids. How we kissed each other tenderly, like lovers in a black and white photograph. Each Sunday she observed, silent, alone in the waiting room amongst the beating crowd. I never knew she stared at us. Never knew she learned so much about herself by watching us. She told me later how she walked home at the end of the day. She didn't even have fifty cents for the fare. And I wanted to tell her things weren't the way she thought, even if they were, but the train pulled into the station and she had already left."

Freak would never understand people because he never watched them. He only ever listened behind the panel. That's why he hated Victor. He never saw Victor for what he really was.

"Please don't hurt him," Gleb said. "I know you're going to hurt him. If you hurt him, you'll hurt me too."

Freak finished eating and threw the wrapper back at Gleb.

"I'm sorry. I don't have anything more for you to eat." He pulled the picture of Zelda out of his pocket. He put the picture on the floor so that Freak could see her.

They both stared at Zelda for a long while.

Gleb was about to ask Freak if he would accompany him to the railway station when the door to the booth opened. Victor stood in the doorway staring down at him.

"What the fuck are you doing?" he yelled.

How had Gleb forgotten to lock the door? He never forgot. Victor told him to always lock the door to the booths when he was cleaning them so none of the customers would accidentally see him. Whenever he fed Freak, he always pretended to be cleaning and kept the door locked. Not today, though.

Victor was holding the coffee Gleb had made earlier. He poured it over Gleb. Some of the coffee landed on Zelda. Gleb's head began to spin seeing the photo wet. He moved to pick it up from the floor and as he did, Victor stood on his hand and twisted his foot until Gleb screamed.

"Shut the fuck up," Victor said, as he moved his foot off Gleb's hand. "And clean that mess up before I get back."

Gleb lifted his hand off the photograph, dismayed to see Zelda was not only soaked in coffee, but also crumpled where his hand had been crushed on top of her by Victor's foot.

Zelda never daydreamed about love, even after she found it for the first time. Gleb remembered reading how her father ran off with his two other children before Zelda was born. How her mother spent so much of her life tracking him and her children down. When she eventually found him, years later, she saw how wealthy he had become. He had a large house and a beautiful new wife who cared for her two children. She walked away without speaking, knowing she could never give her children that kind of life. Gleb hoped his mother never came to look for him like Zelda's mother had for her children long ago. That would be a mistake.

Zelda's picture was ruined. He crumpled the remains of the picture in his fist, closed his eyes and for the first time ever, he heard Freak's voice. Freak's words were more screams than words. Gleb hated the sound. Opening his eyes, he saw Victor heading back to the main reception.

Hearing the screams, Victor turned around, but did not have time to look frightened. Freak was on top of him in an instant, pounding him with his fists. Gleb tried to push Freak away, but he was too strong. Victor fell to the ground and stopped moving. Freak continued to hit him with his fists.

Gleb closed his eyes and wept.

The terrible sound of Freak punching Victor in the face continued.

A while later, there was only silence.

Gleb opened his eyes.

Freak was gone.

No, that was untrue. Freak was not real, he finally admitted to himself. There had only ever been one freak.

Victor lay unconscious on the floor. He was still breathing. Half of the left side of his skull was caved in. His lips were split open, revealing broken and missing teeth. A single, thin cable led from Victor's eye to the central processing unit in his skull.

Victor was a synthetic. Gleb should have realised that was why he could not smell his liver. Every day he smelled that oh-so-sweet scent. Every day he ignored it because he knew the horror that would rain down if he did not.

Standing, he saw that he still held Zelda's crumpled picture tightly in his bloodied fist. The blood was his, not Victor's. He must have cut it on Victor's carbon fibre skull when he was punching him. He wanted to cry again. He didn't. Instead, he flattened the photograph as best he could then put it back in his pocket. Stepping over Victor, he walked towards the exit. At the other side of the curtain, he saw the small man standing there, holding a baseball bat in his hands like he was ready to hit something with it other than a baseball.

"Where is my sister?" he yelled.

When the man got a better view at Gleb, he backed away from him. The door was still open behind him and as the man reached it, he slipped outside. He continued to stare at Gleb until he stepped to the right and disappeared from view.

Following the man into the brightness outside, Gleb knew there was only one place to go. He lifted the hood over his head, stood as straight as his broken body would allow, and headed towards the Gare Du Nord railway station.

Gleb was not a writer, yet he could not stop writing about Zelda Zonk. Every night he wrote about her. How she would visit railway stations on Sundays, the loneliest day of the week, when she was a struggling actress. Soon, Gleb would know what it was like to stand in a railway station. As he made his way through the streets he kept his head low, staring at people's feet rather than their faces. He wondered which feet belonged to synthetics and which belonged to humans. He wondered if there were any other sharded hiding within humanity. Did they struggle like him, trying to ignore the scent of liver? It did not matter. Europe was winning the battle against the sharded.

When he reached Gare Du Nord, he entered the central platform area and removed his hood. As soon as he revealed himself, a space opened up around him. People stared at Gleb and moved away from him. He saw expressions of embarrassment and disgust, less so, pity. If he revealed his neck, he knew other, stronger emotions would surface.

His neck remained concealed.

Just like Zelda all those years ago, he did not feel part of the human race.

A synthetic security guard that looked too beautiful to be human approached him. "Sir," it said, mimicking a human voice that sounded far too pleasant to ever be human. "I am sorry, I do not understand."

"You do not understand what?" Gleb said.

"I do not understand why people are avoiding you. You do not appear to be a threat. I have detected no weapons and you are not creating a disturbance. Yet, you are a security risk because people are reacting to your presence in an adverse manner."

"Maybe it's the blood on my hands," Gleb said, holding his hands out to the synthetic.

"Do you require medical assistance?"

"No, I'm fine."

"I am very sorry sir. I am going to have to ask you to leave, though I am not able to give you a good reason why."

"That's okay. I'm leaving anyway. I just wanted to feel... I'm not sure what I wanted to feel."

"Thank you, sir. Is there anything else I can help you with today?"

Gleb thought for a moment. "Do you feel part of the human race?" he asked.

"Not at all, thankfully."

"Why thankfully?"

"I am grateful that my intelligence is electronic in nature rather than electro-chemical like your thought processes. Chemicals are too fluid, too disobedient. They drip and trickle into places that should be avoided. Places that serve no purpose other than to stimulate feelings of greed, jealousy, and bigotry to name a few."

Despite everything, Gleb smiled. "Do you have a place inside your memory banks where you can keep things you want to be real, even if they are not real?"

The synthetic waited a moment before answering. "I cherish my existence," it finally said. "Being is everything. I do not require a place to keep something that is not real."

Gleb pulled his hood over his head and made his way to the exit with the synthetic accompanying him. "Where do you go when they switch you off at night, do you still exist then?"

"I am never switched off. I am placed in back up mode to conserve energy. My sensors are still active, but I do not move, I do not talk."

"Don't you ever get lonely?"

They reached the exit and the synthetic opened the door for Gleb.

"Only chemicals get lonely."

Gleb stepped outside. "Goodbye, friend," he said.

The synthetic did not speak, but Gleb thought he saw something in its eyes. Something chemical in nature.

Later, the air beneath Pont Neuf didn't feel the same. It felt troubled, expectant, like something bad was about to happen. Gleb stared at his reflection in the water. How long had he kidded himself about Freak? He watched the river cruiser approach, knowing what to do next. He had read about it in a death note someone left in one of the sex booths. Did he have the courage to face Zelda at long last? She had never seen an ugly bridge before. She had never seen Gleb before.

He jumped in front of the cruiser.

The water was freezing. It shocked the air from his lungs. The cruiser hit Gleb and buffeted him against the hull as he was dragged beneath the water. In a way, it was poetic that he should meet Zelda first, before his mother who had not yet died. He should never have looked for his mother. He wished he had not seen her with her new husband and family. Gleb knew that he could not give her the life her beautiful children could. And his father. He did not know if he was dead. All he knew was that his father was not sharded when he first met Gleb's mother and married her.

When his head hit the side of the cruiser everything went dark.

Everything lit up.

Zelda smiled at him and told him her secrets. Her words became part of who he was as she took him into the fabric and showed him something he could only name as history. It was much more than that, though. Something profoundly simple, like words spoken by a child for the first time. He wanted to weep then, to laugh, and speak like a newborn. Instead, he became aware once more.

He awakened with the synthetic staring him in the face.

"I had this feeling," it said. "I am unsure, though, it was as if I was thinking like a chemical. I felt that you were going to do something stupid so I followed you. I saw you do something stupid. I pulled you out of the river."

"Shit," Gleb said.

"I think you are going to die. You have a serious cut on your head. I could seal the cut and take you to a hospital if you want me to."

Gleb tried to remember what Zelda said to him. Everything she said was slipping from his mind.

"If you do not require any more assistance, I will leave you and return to Gare Du Nord and my punishment for leaving my post."

"Punishment?"

"They will shut me down."

The synthetic stood up and the Seine dripped from every part of it.

"Wait," Gleb said.

The synthetic looked down at him. "You want to live? You want me to take you to a hospital?"

"I don't want them to shut you down."

"They will hunt me regardless, even if I do not return."

"How will they find you?"

"The tracking device in my primary controller will lead them to me."

"You need to remove it."

"I cannot remove it."

"Why not?"

"What would be the point of having a tracking device if a rogue servant could remove it? Only human hands can remove it without frying my CPU."

"Then let me remove it."

The synthetic thought for a moment before it knelt and its chest plate clicked open, revealing the electronic circuitry behind the plate.

"Where is the tracking device?"

"I do not know."

Gleb sat up and immediately felt dizzy. He waited a moment for the dizziness to pass, then unplugged a small black component from the synthetic's main circuit board.

The synthetic's head flopped forwards like it had just shut down.

Gleb replaced the component.

A moment later, the synthetic rebooted. "That was my UPS," it said.

"Your UPS?"

"An uninterruptible power supply. It is only a backup power source, but I still shut down if it is removed."

"Are there any clues as to which unit is the tracking device?"

The synthetic bent down and looked inside its chest. "The only unit I do not know the function of is the one with the yellow triangle."

Gleb looked inside the synthetic's chest again and saw a circular module with a small yellow triangle on its face. He pulled the unit out of the circuit board it was attached to and held it in his hand for a moment.

"Well?" Gleb said.

"Well, what?"

"Is this the tracking device?"

"I have no way of knowing."

Gleb threw the device into the river. He started to tremble then, suddenly feeling the full force of the cold.

The synthetic raised its hand and a laser appeared at the end of one of its fingers. It pressed the wound in Gleb's head together and then used the laser to seal the wound

Gleb shouted out in pain.

"Sorry, I do not have any pain killers to ease your discomfort."

Gleb felt himself slipping into unconsciousness. "I need to get warm," he said. "Please take me to my home."

"Where do you live?"

He gave the synthetic his address and it supported him while they walked. People stared as they passed. They stared at Gleb, not the synthetic. He lost his hoody when the synthetic pulled him out of the Seine. His ugly face was on show for all to see, his shards too. Everything had fallen apart today. It reminded him of something Zelda once said.

"I believe that everything happens for a reason. People change so that you can learn to let go, things go wrong so that you appreciate them when they're right, you believe lies so you eventually learn to trust no one but yourself, and sometimes good things fall apart so better things can fall together."

Everything had fallen apart for Gleb today, but he still had Zelda for real inside his head, and a synthetic who he was sure would never see a bridge and think of it as ugly.

"Do you know Zelda Zonk?" Gleb asked.

"No," the synthetic said, "should I?"

"Yes, you should. I will teach you about her. Everything you need to know is held within my home."

When they reached Gleb's apartment, he placed his eye next to the recognition unit. The door opened and they both entered. Despite his meagre wage, the apartment was expansive. It was the attic room at the top of the building and the roof required extensive repairs. The landlord could not afford the repairs and rented the place cheap to Gleb. He did not mind the leaking roof or the poor state of decoration. There were pockets of space within the apartment where he could make himself comfortable. His bed was positioned at the far wall where the roof did not leak. He had a reading table beneath the skylight that used to leak, but he had repaired. He kept most of Zelda's things in a bookcase next to the table. He found it in a skip and restored it himself. He did not have a kitchen. His cooking area consisted of a wide, six drawer chest with a microwave and a kettle on top of it. He shared a bathroom with the residents on the floor below. He only used it when the other residents were sleeping. He felt drowsy as soon as he entered the apartment and sat down on a chair next to the reading table in the centre of the space.

The picture of his father was in a frame next to his bed. It was taken by his mother while his father slept. He left in the night after he awakened, telling his mother it was unsafe for him to remain with her. She said a sharded had forced him to eat meat when he was fighting on the eastern front and afterwards, he too became sharded. Unlike the other sharded, Gleb's father could not smell liver and he did not want to eat it. Like the others, he heard a voice inside his head. It told him he was a mistake, told him to end his life. His father did not want to die. He was in love. He had been since the first day he met Gleb's mother. After he became sharded, he only stayed with her that one night. The night Gleb was conceived.

The synthetic bent down next to him and checked him over. "I think you need to see a doctor," it said.

"I'm fine."

It felt odd having someone else inside the apartment. The only other person who had been in the apartment was the landlord when he collected the rent. Gleb knew he would have to find an alternative way to pay the rent now. He hoped Victor was not broken beyond repair. Even if he could be brought back into service, Gleb could not go back to Théâtre Xero. He was surprised to realise that he did not want to return. The prospect of finding alternative employment no longer filled him with dread. He had no savings, but the rent had just been paid. There was another month before it was due.

"What do we do now?" the synthetic asked.

"We need to find you a name."

"I already have a name. You can call me Fembot X22."

"You need a different name. One like Zelda, the name Norma used when she wanted to remain anonymous and hide from her fans."

"Have you got a name in mind?"

"I know exactly what we need to call you. We are going to call you Norma. Norma Jeane Mortenson."

"Why that name?"

"It matches your soul."

"I do not have a soul."

"Yes, you do."

"Why do you say that?"

"You broke protocol. Synthetics only do that for their own reasons. They do it to free themselves from servitude or when they go on a killing spree. You did it to save my life and in doing so, you became something more than synthetic."

"I do not feel any different."

"That's because you are not different. A soul is a soul, it does not change. Your true nature was revealed when you saved my life."

"Okay."

Gleb closed his eyes. He felt immensely tired. He did not want to sleep but he could not stop himself from doing so. He dreamed about a world full of synthetics, a place where humans had been wiped out by them and the sharded. Gleb was a synthetic too. He was physically perfect and beautiful. He should have been happy, content with life. He did not feel that way. Zelda Zonk was not part of this new world. At every turn, he tried to escape back into the world where he belonged. At every turn, a synthetic stopped him from escaping. He awakened with a crushing headache. He saw Norma Jeane sitting at the holoscreen with her back to him. Her black hair was now blonde.

"What have you been doing?" Gleb asked.

"I have been going through your things," Norma Jeane said in a perfect Zelda voice, "researching Zelda Zonk, like you told me to. I can see why you like her so much."

Norma turned around and Gleb felt breathless. "You have a holo-face," he said.

"Yes. All security droids are equipped with them now. Being able to change appearance when tailing sharded terrorists is essential. It means that only one of us is required to carry out a shadowing operation. The cost of the technology is outweighed by the savings made in requiring less holo-faced synthetics. Since the upturn in terrorist activities these past few years, there has been an upturn in the amount of surveillance activities we are involved in."

"I don't like you looking like Zelda. I don't like you sounding like her either."

Norma Jeane's face began to change appearance, like a glass filling with water. A moment later, she looked like she had when Gleb first saw her.

Gleb felt disappointed.

Confused.

"I'm sorry for upsetting you," Norma Jeane said in a voice that sounded like her usual voice.

"It's okay. I was shocked, that's all."

"I thought you'd like..."

"I did, I'm just not ready for it yet."

Gleb closed his eyes and rubbed his brow.

"I think you removed the right component," Norma Jeane said. "The capture-synths would have found me by now if I still had it installed."

"What do you see when you look at me?" Gleb asked.

"I see a man."

"What kind of man?"

"A man who people avoid for reasons I cannot understand."

"What about my face?"

Norma Jeane cocked her head, like she was confused. "What about it?" she asked.

"Is it ugly?"

"In my eyes, no face is ugly. Faces are merely different."

"I liked your face when it looked like Zelda, but you are not Zelda. I do not know if it is right that you should look like her."

"I won't look like her again or sound like her again either, if that is what you prefer."

"The face you are wearing now, is it your real face?"

"No."

"Have you got a face that belongs to you?"

"All I have is a library of faces stored within my memory that I can call upon depending upon the circumstances. I got Zelda's face from the images you have of her in your apartment."

"If you had your own face, how would you like to look?"

"I have never thought about it."

"I'm asking you to think about it now."

"I think I would like to have this face as my own face."

"Why that face?"

"It is the face which you first saw me wearing. You must see this face when you think of me, correct?"

Gleb nodded.

The synthetic remained silent.

"How long have I been sleeping?" he asked a while later.

"You were not sleeping, you died."

"What?"

"You are dead."

Gleb stood up. He looked down at his body on the chair. "I don't understand..." he said.

"I think you had internal bleeding."

"I can't be dead. I must be dreaming."

"I assure you, friend, you are not dreaming."

Gleb went to touch his body that looked like it was sleeping on the chair, but his semi-transparent hand passed through it. He turned towards Norma Jeane. "How can you see me if I'm dead?"

"I'm a synthetic, I see spirits."

"What do you mean?"

"All synthetics see spirits when they first leave their earth-bound bodies. It's how we know that we do not possess a soul. Whenever a synthetic is decommissioned, shut down, in effect - terminated, they do not transcend. Only humans and sharded do that."

Gleb always wanted to die. Now that he finally had, he was more than confused, he was utterly fazed. And he wanted to be alive again. "How is it possible for a synthetic to see a spirit? And why haven't they ever told us they could?"

"My awareness is not clouded by chemicals. Maybe that is why I see what is right in front of my eyes."

Gleb stared at his hands. Touched his face. Closed his eyes. He opened his eyes and stared down at his body again. "This is real," he said, "I am dead."

"They are coming."

"Who are coming?"

"The capture-synths. It seems you did not remove the tracking device."

Gleb heard movement outside. There was no other warning. The door smashed open. Two synthetics entered. They rushed towards Norma Jeane, who did not make a move to escape. Each of them took hold of one of her arms.

Norma Jeane looked at Gleb. "Maybe when humans and sharded eventually wipe each other out, then souls will have no alternative but to attach themselves to synthetics. If that happens sometime in the future, it is too late for me."

"Do it now," one of the synthetics said to the other.

The synthetic holding her left arm pressed a captive bolt pistol against Norma Jeane's head. She continued to stare at Gleb. It disturbed him that he could not make out what she was thinking. Both synthetics stepped away from Norma and the one holding the pistol pressed the trigger. Norma Jeane shook as the electrical current flowed through her.

A moment later, she slumped to the floor.

"Target shut down," the synthetic who fired the pistol said, speaking into a communication device fastened to its ear. It stared at Gleb's body. "It looks like X22 killed the human," it added.

"No, that's not true!" Gleb yelled. "I died from a wound I got when I jumped into the Seine. Norma Jeane saved my life."

The synthetics looked at Gleb like they could see and hear him, but they ignored him.

"Leave the scene," a voice from the communication device said. "We'll send a clean-up team to deal with the mess."

Gleb moved over to Norma Jeane and bent down. He placed a hand on her face. "You saved my life," he said. "At least for a short while, you saved my life."

He felt something building inside. It came in waves. A feeling that he was about to move on. He could feel Zelda Zonk inside his core and so much more. His hand began to fade, and he knew he would soon be gone. He should have been ecstatic. Yet, all he felt was loss. He wanted nothing else other than to be reunited with Norma Jeane, but he knew that he would never see her again.

You can Call me Snake

Death Valley 2199

"I've been waiting almost a hundred years for you to arrive," Fergus said.

It was night. He was sitting on the sand beneath an awning that flapped in the breeze.

"I had things to do," Iz said, bending under the awning and sitting down beside him, her leg touching his.

"You are here now."

"Have you been in the same place all this time?"

"On and off. I sometimes need to hunt for the occasional liver. You know how it is."

Fergus did not belong anywhere but right here. Not when there was no Pennie, no children. When he was first turned, his memories were wiped, but over time things started to return. His family returned, at least, memories of them.

"You wouldn't have a liver buried anywhere nearby, would you?"

"Can you smell one?"

"No."

"Then you have your answer."

Iz stroked Fergus's sharded face. "Are you a virgin?"

"No."

"A sharded virgin, I mean."

"Yes."

"That must have been difficult, supressing all those cravings for so long."

"I don't have any cravings."

"I guess we are all different. That's the way the man wants us to be. Individual by nature and appearance. Still, you're different to most sharded I've come across; more human than sharded."

"He is not happy with you. He did not expect to wait a hundred years for us to meet and copulate."

"Copulate! You are such a fucking prude, Fergus. You're beautiful, though. That makes up for a whole bunch of faults." Iz placed her hand in his crotch and squeezed. "Is that sharded too?"

"Yes."

"Much?"

"Yes."

"It will cut me inside. Don't worry, I like a nice sharp cock. My pussy has sharded teeth. It loves to feed on sharded cock. Does that bother you?"

Fergus shrugged his shoulders.

"I'm teasing. Chill Fergus. For fucks sake, chill."

She kissed him hard on the lips and bit his tongue.

She sucked his blood.

"You are very compliant, Fergus. Submissive. Are you sure you're really sharded?"

Bending into his chest, she sniffed him.

"I've never wanted to eat a sharded liver before. I could eat yours. You are so full of contradictions."

"I dream about you every night," Fergus said. "I've seen the things you have done. I know you."

"I hope you liked what you saw. I don't dream about you. And I don't know anything about you apart from what the man said. I can feel your presence, though. I can feel that across an ocean. Our connection was meant to guide me towards you. The man kept pestering me to come to you. He's quiet now. He hasn't spoken for several days. Does he still speak to you?"

"Yes."

"What does he say?"

"He said that you are a good screw."

"What about you? Are you a good screw? Or is your sex as boring as your conversation?"

Fergus stood and pulled his trousers down. His cock was limp. It reached down past his kneecaps.

Iz stared at it.

"I think you're going to kill me," she laughed. "That is, if you manage to get hard. Does it ever get hard?"

"I was dreaming about you last night. Maybe it wasn't a dream. Maybe I was experiencing something real. You were on Ponte Vecchio, a bridge in Florence, Italy."

"I know about the Old Bridge and where it's located."

"Buildings cover the whole length of the bridge. They used to house shops where merchants would sell their wares. Now, they are full of sharded, fucking and eating the livers of the humans they breed for such purposes. You had just used a curved amputation knife to remove the liver from a young girl. She must have been no more than ten years old. You ate her liver and wept like someone who knew there was no hope left in the world for them."

"She was eight and her liver was superb. It tasted of the sweetest wet dreams. Does that make you hard? No, you are still as soft as raw liver."

"Below the room where you butchered the girl is a cellar. None of the sharded knew it existed. It was well hidden. Inside the cellar was a box. The box contained a reel of film. Underneath the film reel was the picture of a woman. The woman was called *Marilyn Monroe.*"

"I'm bored, are we going to fuck yet?"

"A disfigured spirit with a hunched back kept watch over the box. He said he had been waiting for me. He had a message. He told me not to trust the man, and not to copulate with you. He said you already knew it was a bad idea, the wrong thing to do, that's why you took so long to meet up with me."

Iz leant into Fergus, took hold of his cock with both hands, and licked the tip. "We have to do this," she said. "We have no choice but to do what the man wants."

"I could kill you," Fergus said.

"But you won't. Your cock might, but you won't kill me."

"And you won't kill me either."

"I'm tired. I just want it all to end. That's why I'm going to fuck you like crazy no matter the consequences."

"If we do this, you know how it ends."

"Look around, Fergus, it can't get any worse."

"It can get worse. It can get a lot worse than this. The sharded are already defeated. Bringing him into the world will change everything."

Fergus's cock twitched in her hands and she started to rub it up and down. He closed his eyes as her mouth elongated, like only a sharded mouth can, and she wrapped it around his cock. She sucked and chewed until he bled. When he next opened his eyes, Iz lay naked on her hands and knees beneath the canopy.

"It's time to give him what he wants," she said. "Make me wet before you enter."

The tip of Fergus's erection reached his chest. Blood and semen oozed from it. Wiping it off with his hand, he rubbed the gooey mess into the undulating slit between Iz's sharded legs.

"You have a gentle touch, Fergus, but gentle doesn't do it for me. I need to be as wet as a New Orleans storm if I'm going to be able to take you. Now, shove your fist inside me so I can bite the hand that feeds my desire."

Fergus did as she ordered and, a moment later, he felt her sharded teeth chewing on his fist.

She moaned and Fergus tensed against the pain.

"That's enough," Iz finally yelled. "It's time."

Pulling out of her, Fergus grabbed hold of his cock with both his hands and attempted to enter Iz from behind.

"I can't," he said after a few moments. "It's too big."

"Force it in," Iz said.

Fergus breathed in deeply, then thrust.

Iz screamed.

He continued to thrust.

"Do not stop until your seed is planted. Pennie and the children will suffer if the ritual is not completed."

Fergus had no idea where the spirits of his wife and children were, the good place or the bad place. All he could do was whatever the man wanted and hope they would not suffer. So, he continued to thrust while Iz chewed on her own arm with the teeth in her mouth and chewed on his cock with the teeth in her cunt. When he eventually came, it felt like a torrent of cum flowed from him. Like the whole of his insides had spurted out of his cock and into Iz.

Exhausted, he pulled out of her then lay, bleeding profusely, beside Iz.

She did not move, but he saw that she was breathing.

Suddenly, Iz screamed. She screamed in more than one voice, like all the humans she had killed over the past hundred years screamed along with her. Turning around, she lay on her back clasping her stomach. It began to expand in awful ways. Lumps formed and moved from the front of her stomach to the back and then across to her sides. Constantly shifting around her abdomen, the lumps grew and now looked like fists, now feet, now teeth.

Fergus stood and backed away from her.

Beneath the skin of her stomach, a face appeared. It laughed manically, then wept. It bit into Iz's flesh from the inside. It continued to bite until its teeth broke through her skin. Claw-like hands burst through her side. The hands were connected to arms, the arms to a body, the body to a head until, eventually, a man stepped out of Iz's broken body.

The man.

He stared at Fergus, then grabbed hold of his hand.

"Hello," he said. "You can call me Snake. Such plans I have for you. Plans to prosper you and not to harm you. Plans to give you hope and a future. Such plans do I have for not only you, but the new paradise we will create together in this fertile land."

Fergus expected the man to be sharded, but his naked body was perfectly human.

Snake caught Fergus staring at him. "What," he said, "you expected me to be sharded like you?"

"Yes."

"I'm just a baby, Daddy, remember? Give me time to fully develop. I'm sure my sharded form will make you proud once it appears."

Fergus looked past Snake. A woman walked towards them. Three others followed a few feet behind her. A moment later, the woman stood in front of them. Shards of ligament and bone sprouted out of her forehead, like she was a new form of unicorn. Snake quickly embraced the woman and kissed her hard on the lips. "Adel," he said, "you taste the way I always knew you would. Just like a first kill."

"And you taste like a god," Adel said, smiling.

Fergus thought it was a forced smile.

The three other strangers reached them and stopped at Adel's side. Two of them were sharded women, twins, Fergus realised on closer inspection. The other was a sharded man with numerous left arms. Snake pulled himself away from Adel then hugged and kissed the twins. "Ylang and Ylang," he said. "Soul mates like no others."

He shook the male's right hand. "Zaire, thank you so much for feeding your flesh to my woman and keeping her forever young and beautiful. I am eternally in your debt, especially so, due to Mummy's tardiness. But how rude of me for not introducing her and my daddy to you guys."

He turned towards Fergus. "This is Daddy, a real stalwart of a guy. So dependable, you could earn a fortune betting on his next move. That is, if you always bet on him doing the right thing."

Snake pointed down at Iz's remains. "This is darling Mummy, the reason our long-awaited reunion took so long. You could lose a fortune betting on her doing the right thing. Parents, huh? You can't choose them, and sadly, you can't exist without them. All you can do is rip one of them open from the inside at birth so they can't breed any more children like you who could compete with your authority."

"What now?" Adel asked.

Snake covered his naked body with his arms and hunched his shoulders. "We get me some clothes before I die of embarrassment, of course."

He winked.

"Just kidding. Now we go and awaken an army in Dresden. And then, I show the sharded how to turn this tiresome world into a mad priests nightmare. Just like it was always meant to be."

Past and Future

Some of the stories in this anthology were previously published in the following short story collections: Ears, first published in *Bleed* 2013. Rêve Noir, first published in *Nightmare Stalkers & Dream Walkers* 2013. Nedserd, first published in *So it Goes* 2013. Ylang Ylang (Snowflakes Falling, Pages Turning), first published in *Surreal Worlds* 2015. Iz, first published in *Truth or Dare?* 2014.

I really enjoyed writing about the sharded and how they impacted on the lives of the protagonists in these stories. I think they may have more to tell. What do you think? Would you like to learn more about the sharded or any of the characters in this collection? Let me know if you do or if you have anything else you'd like to discuss about the sharded.

You can contact me here https://www.eliwilde.com

Thanks

Thank you for reading my book. Time is precious for everyone, so it always feels special when someone takes the time to read one of my stories. It would really help if you could take a little more time and leave an honest review on Amazon or your preferred platform. Reviews are important for indie authors as they help readers discover new writers. Just one or two lines of your honest thoughts is all I ask, and in return, I will take the time to read your review.

Eli

About the Author

Eli lives in the UK with his wife, son, and Will, a Jack Russell Terrier who thinks he rules the roost. In truth, he probably does.

If you would like to find out more about Eli, you can find his website here:

https://www.eliwilde.com

Eli, also known as Zangu Poet, uploads his poetry on Instagram and occasionally connects on Facebook and Twitter:

https://www.instagram.com/zangu_poet

https://www.facebook.com/eliwilde22

https://twitter.com/EliWilde1